W9-BZP-850

# "*Don't you touch me!*"

"You're surely not *frightened* of me?"

Of course she wasn't frightened. Except of her own reactions. She was disgusted.

Wasn't she?

"You're totally unscrupulous, aren't you?" she accused him.

"I've never thought so," he said. "It was only a kiss. An impulse. I'm sorry if you're offended."

A master of understatement. It didn't help that she could still taste his mouth on hers, still feel the imprint of his body.

As if he knew it, he said, "I didn't get the impression that it was unwelcome... at first."

*DAPHNE CLAIR* lives in Aotearoa, New Zealand, with her Dutch-born husband. Their five children have left home but drift back at irregular intervals. At eight years old she embarked on her first novel, about taming a tiger. This epic never reached a publisher, but metamorphosed male tigers still prowl the pages of her romances. Her other writing includes nonfiction, poetry and short stories, and she has won literary prizes in New Zealand and America.

## Books by Daphne Clair

**HARLEQUIN PRESENTS PLUS**
1648—FLAME ON THE HORIZON

**HARLEQUIN PRESENTS**
711—TAKE HOLD OF TOMORROW
881—DARK DREAM
1056—NO ESCAPE
1096—NO WINNER
1271—THE WAYWARD BRIDE
1586—AND THEN CAME MORNING

**HARLEQUIN ROMANCE**
2197—A STREAK OF GOLD
2292—THE SLEEPING FIRE
2329—THE JASMINE BRIDE
2420—NEVER COUNT TOMORROW
2516—PACIFIC PRETENCE

Don't miss any of our special offers. Write to us at the following address for information on our newest releases.

Harlequin Reader Service
U.S.: 3010 Walden Ave., P.O. Box 1325, Buffalo, NY 14269
Canadian: P.O. Box 609, Fort Erie, Ont. L2A 5X3

# Daphne *Clair*

# DARK MIRROR

## *Harlequin Books*

TORONTO • NEW YORK • LONDON
AMSTERDAM • PARIS • SYDNEY • HAMBURG
STOCKHOLM • ATHENS • TOKYO • MILAN
MADRID • WARSAW • BUDAPEST • AUCKLAND

If you purchased this book without a cover you should be aware
that this book is stolen property. It was reported as "unsold and
destroyed" to the publisher, and neither the author nor the
publisher has received any payment for this "stripped book."

ISBN 0-373-11688-8

DARK MIRROR

Copyright © 1994 by Daphne de Jong.

All rights reserved. Except for use in any review, the reproduction or
utilization of this work in whole or in part in any form by any electronic,
mechanical or other means, now known or hereafter invented, including
xerography, photocopying and recording, or in any information storage
or retrieval system, is forbidden without the written permission of the
publisher, Harlequin Enterprises Limited, 225 Duncan Mill Road,
Don Mills, Ontario, Canada M3B 3K9.

All characters in this book have no existence outside the imagination of
the author and have no relation whatsoever to anyone bearing the same
name or names. They are not even distantly inspired by any individual
known or unknown to the author, and all incidents are pure invention.

This edition published by arrangement with Harlequin Enterprises B. V.

® and TM are trademarks of the publisher. Trademarks indicated with
® are registered in the United States Patent and Trademark Office, the
Canadian Trade Marks Office and in other countries.

Printed in U.S.A.

# CHAPTER ONE

THE man was standing in the hospital corridor when Fler came out of the room where they'd put her daughter. They'd told her he was there, that he'd brought Tansy in. She couldn't recall whether he'd been there when she arrived. She'd been too intent then on getting to Tansy's side, finding out her chances, being there for her, to notice anyone—anything—that wasn't directly related to her daughter's survival.

Now she smelled the antiseptic and polish, saw the cheap prints on the walls and the shine of the green vinyl on the wide floor of the corridor, heard the murmur of voices from the ward office. And saw the tall, grey-suited man straighten from where he'd been leaning against the wall with his arms folded, and come towards her.

With a curious detachment she noted the thick brown hair, brushed neatly back, the slight furrow between his dark brows, the hazel eyes and pronounced cheekbones, the cheeks appearing rather hollowed by contrast. His nose was classically straight but a shade long, and his mouth wasn't thin but looked firm and decisive. There was something surprising about that mouth.

He looked older than she'd expected, and briefly she wondered if she was mistaken, but he said, 'Mrs Hewson? My name's Kyle Ranburn...' And she knew there was no mistake.

He seemed surprised too, she noticed. From being oblivious to her surroundings, she'd suddenly become hypersensitive to every irrelevant detail. A nurse walked by them, and she heard the hushed squeak of rubber on the well-shined floor. She noticed that Kyle Ranburn wore no tie, that his rumpled shirt had three buttons undone, and a pulse was beating under the lightly tanned skin of his throat, revealed by the open collar. His eyes were flecked with brown around the irises, more green towards the edge. And he hadn't shaved. A musky male scent underlaid the faint sharpness of sweat. He probably hadn't had a chance to wash, either. She supposed she ought to be grateful that he had obviously lost no time answering Tansy's call in the night.

He held out a hand to her and she looked down at it, saw his fingers were long but blunt-ended, the nails cut short.

When she didn't take his hand, he withdrew it, saying evenly, 'How is she now?'

'They think they've got rid of the pills. She'll probably be all right, if there's no liver damage. They're going to keep her in for a couple of days to be sure. But they seem fairly sure they got the drugs out of her system in time. She isn't going to die.'

'That's good.'

'You must be relieved?' Fler asked in brittle tones.

'Yes, of course. Very.' Unforgivably, he glanced at the leather-strapped stainless steel watch on his wrist. 'Look, I really have to go, I'm afraid——'

The gesture broke her determined calm. All the varied emotions she'd been tightly reining in for hours, while she hastily dressed in anything that came to hand, made hurried phone calls of her own, ran to her car in the cold dawn and then drove for almost three long, terrified hours, shattered in a flare of shaking, white-hot rage. '*You callous bastard*!' She wanted to hit him, preferably with a blunt instrument.

He blinked. 'I'm sorry——'

'I'm sure you are!'

He looked away for a moment, as if thinking, and then said, 'I don't know what Tansy told you, Mrs Hewson, but——'

'She's told me about you!'

'—I didn't do anything to her. She did it to herself.'

'You know damned well you were responsible!' Tansy's broken, tearful, half-conscious mutterings had made that unmistakably clear. 'How old are you?'

He looked taken aback. 'What?'

'I said, how old are you? You must have known that Tansy is only eighteen.'

'If that has anything to do with——'

'You must be at least ten years older.'

'I'm thirty,' he said. 'Look, Mrs Hewson, Tansy has a problem——'

'Yes, she does. You!'

He ran a hand over his hair, and looked about them. An orderly was wheeling a frail, grey-haired man down the corridor towards them, and two nurses came through the swing doors and walked past, chattering. 'This isn't really the place to discuss it. And I do have to go.'

'I don't think I have anything to discuss with you,' Fler said. 'Thank you for bringing Tansy in,' she added stiffly. He'd probably saved her life. But it wouldn't have needed saving if this man had any sense of decency, if Tansy had never had the misfortune to meet him.

He looked as though he wanted to say something more, but then he made an exasperated gesture with his hands, nodded to her curtly, and left.

'Would you like a cup of coffee?' the nurse coming out of Tansy's room offered.

She shook her head. 'May I go back and sit with my daughter?'

'Yes, of course. She's sleeping it off now. Not likely to wake again for some time. Maybe you should get yourself something to eat at the cafeteria.'

'I will later,' she promised. Just now she had to be with Tansy, hold her hand and feel its inert warmth in hers, assure herself that her daughter was really breathing, really alive after that brush with deliberately induced death.

She could scarcely believe that lovely, bright, talented Tansy, with all her future before her, had really tried to kill herself.

They said she'd emptied the medicine cupboard in the bathroom of the flat she shared with three other students, all of them away for the weekend. She'd taken everything she found. The medical team had managed to get that much information from her, and from the man she'd finally called before the cocktail of drugs she'd swallowed took deadly effect. He'd had the sense to collect up the bottles and bring them into the hospital with her.

'She's lucky,' they said. 'He did all the right things.'

It didn't make her feel any more kindly towards Kyle Ranburn. What must the man have done to poor Tansy, to make her so desperate?

And why, darling, Fler thought, staring at the pathetically tangled fair hair on the pillow and the waxy pallor of her daughter's face, why didn't you call me, tell me what was troubling you? Whatever it was, we'd have worked it out. We will, when you're better, she promised silently. And found tears running hotly down her cheeks.

There was a basin in the small room, and she got up to rinse away the tears. It wouldn't help Tansy for her to crack up now.

She splashed cold water over her face and dried it with a paper towel. In the mirror over the basin she looked almost as white as the girl in the bed, her clear green eyes dulled and bloodshot with worry and the aftermath of tears. Her hair, several shades darker than Tansy's, was a mess. Automatically she took a comb from her bag and smoothed it back over her ears in the sleek style she'd adopted when she got it cut a few years ago.

Tansy had objected. 'I liked it long.'

'It's a nuisance,' Fler had told her. 'I have to pin it up every day, and I haven't got the time.'

'Leave it loose,' Tansy had suggested. 'It's pretty.'

'I'm too old for that.'

'Thirty-four isn't all that old,' fifteen-year-old Tansy had assured her endearingly. 'And anyway, you don't look it.'

She was thirty-seven now, and this morning she looked every day of it, she was sure. The fine lines at the corners of her eyes and on her forehead were more pronounced than usual, and there were blue shadows beneath her eyes. Even her mouth was pale. She fumbled a lipstick from the bag and used it. If Tansy woke soon, she wouldn't want to find her mother looking as though she was in need of a hospital bed herself.

She closed the bag and went back to the bed, gazing at the oblivious girl for a few minutes, then going to the window to stare out at the view, what there was of it.

A hum of morning traffic rose from the invisible streets of Auckland. Several floors down she could see people hurrying from a car park to the hospital buildings, some of the women wearing white or green uniforms, most clutching jackets or coats against a wintry breeze, although the sun glinted off the windows of the parked cars. Between a jumble of anonymous tower blocks she glimpsed a few round-headed trees, and in the distance a wedge of blue sea.

She'd take Tansy home, she thought. Home to Northland, away from Auckland and its impersonal big-city atmosphere. Away from men like Kyle Ranburn.

Kyle Ranburn. A name that months before had begun to crop up with disturbing regularity in Tansy's infrequent letters, her rather more frequent collect calls home. At first Fler had thought he was a fellow student. It was some time before she'd discovered he was on the staff of the university, before she had begun to be uneasy about his influence on her daughter, and Tansy's obvious dependence on him.

Before she'd realised that her daughter was engaged in a full-blown love-affair with a man who, she became increasingly certain, was probably enjoying having an ardent, inexperienced young girl on a string but who was bound eventually to break her heart.

When Tansy was home for the May holidays, Fler had tried tactfully to voice her concern.

'I know you think a great deal of this man,' she said. 'But he must be a few years older than you. What sort of person is he?'

Apparently he was some kind of demigod, from Tansy's rapturous description. But it didn't really tell her much.

When the eulogy appeared to be over she said, keeping her voice light, 'I expect half of your friends have a crush on him, too, if he's as wonderful as you say.'

'You don't understand,' Tansy declared impatiently, the age-old pronouncement of youth to a parent. 'It's not like that at all. Kyle and I have a ... a relationship.'

A relationship? Did she mean——? 'What kind of relationship?' she asked.

Mistake. She'd meant it to sound like a matter-of-fact woman-to-woman question. It had come out sharply, almost an accusation, definitely mother-to-possibly-wayward-daughter. 'Are you going out together?' she asked more casually.

'Sometimes. Well, we don't exactly go *out* much, you know. I see him in class, of course, and he takes some of the tutorials himself. But Kyle has to be careful. Discreet, you know? He couldn't let anyone think he's favouring me. He's got to think of his position.'

Does he, now? Fler thought grimly. It sounded as though Tansy was quoting him. He didn't want to be seen with her in public. That was obvious. 'You know, it's not exactly ethical for a lecturer to seduce one of his students,' she said.

'Kyle hasn't *seduced* me!'

Maybe not yet, but Fler would have laid odds it was on his agenda. With the emphasis Tansy had given it, the remark was ambiguous. She asked a blunt question. 'Are you sleeping with him?'

'What if I am?' Tansy flushed, looking boldly at her mother. 'I'm over the age of consent, so there isn't a thing you can do about it.'

That gave Fler a nasty little jolt. She said, 'How serious is this, Tansy?'

'I love him,' Tansy said, her eyes wide and defiant.

As gently as she could, Fler said, 'Darling, are you sure you're not fooling yourself?'

Tansy had been immediately defensive and angry, and they'd had their first major quarrel in years. It had ended with Tansy in tears, accusing Fler of not wanting to let go of the apron strings, of being jealous of her daughter having a man when she didn't, of wanting to ruin Tansy's life as she'd wrecked her own.

Of course Fler had taken it all with a healthy pinch of salt. Tansy was still young and didn't mean half of what she said in temper. But the accusations were a disturbing echo of her own insecurities. Maybe there was a grain of truth in them. So she'd trodden carefully from then on, wary of alienating Tansy, terribly afraid for her, and holding herself ready to be available for comfort and support when the inevitable break finally came.

Now it had, with stunning force. Never in a million years would she have expected Tansy to attempt suicide. She felt sick with shock. And guilty, too. Because she hadn't foreseen anything like this, although she'd thought she and Tansy were close.

But mostly, she felt a hot, vengeful rage against the man who had carelessly, cruelly, for some whim or because it fed his masculine ego, brought her lovely, loving daughter to the brink of self-destruction. Quite simply, she wanted to kill him.

# CHAPTER TWO

'KYLE?'

Tansy's voice was scarcely more than a whisper.

Fler instantly crossed to the bed, her anxious eyes on the gold-tipped lashes struggling to open. 'Tansy...' She took the slack hand again in hers, smoothed the fine hair away from the clammy forehead. 'It's all right, I'm here.'

Tansy's brow briefly wrinkled. She managed to open her eyes for a moment before they closed heavily. 'Mummy!' The old childhood name. 'Wha' are you...?'

'The hospital called me.' The early morning call, the calm, impersonal voice on the line... 'Your daughter has been brought into hospital...an overdose...'

'Where' Kyle?' Tansy whispered.

Fler tamped down a fresh spasm of rage. Calmly she said, 'He had to go. Don't worry about it now.'

A tear appeared under the closed lashes and ran on to the pillow. Fler said almost fiercely, 'Don't cry, darling! Everything's going to be all right. You'll see.'

I *will* kill him, she thought dispassionately. One of these days I damned well will.

As a serious proposition, the resolution faded overnight. Regretfully, Fler acknowledged that she wasn't the stuff of which murderers were made. It didn't stop her from fantasising about doing serious harm to Kyle Ranburn. More realistically, she contemplated laying a complaint with the university authorities, but knew that her own relationship with Tansy might suffer badly from that. And what Tansy needed now was support and rest, not to be unwillingly involved in a vendetta which might well turn public.

It made her heart ache that every time she went into the room she saw the tense expectancy in Tansy's face turn momentarily to disappointment before she put on a smile for her mother. Neither of them mentioned Kyle Ranburn again, but he was always, Fler was grimly aware, there in spirit, like a spectre at the feast.

The staff told her he hadn't visited, and although she was sure that it was better for Tansy not to see him again she was furious all over again at his heartlessness. She covertly inspected the card on a basket of flowers that appeared on the bedside locker late on Sunday, but it was from Tansy's flatmates.

That evening, when they had told her that Tansy would be discharged in the morning, she found him at the ward door when she was on her way out.

She halted abruptly at the sight of him, and said, 'Have you come to see her at last?'

He shook his head. He looked grim and slightly uncomfortable. As well he might, she thought.

'No,' he said. 'Actually I hoped to see you.'

Her head went up sharply. 'Why?'

'I thought . . . we should talk about your daughter.'

A group of visitors brushed past them, carrying flowers and magazines, and he lightly took her arm, moving her to one side.

Fler pulled away from him, her mouth tight.

He said, 'Can I buy you a cup of coffee? Somewhere that we can talk with a bit of privacy.'

She said, 'I'll buy my own coffee, thanks.' She didn't want to take anything from this man. 'But I'd like to talk to you, too.' She had a few home truths to tell him.

*     *     *

They walked to a coffee bar. He seemed to know the area, and while the place he chose wasn't upmarket it was clean and cosy and the coffee was good. He led her to a booth and saw her seated before he slid in opposite her. He asked her what the doctors had said, and she told him that they didn't expect any permanent after-effects.

He nodded and said formally, 'I'm glad. That must be a burden lifted for you.'

Fler didn't answer. The booth was small, and she was conscious of his masculine aura, a sense of controlled power, of assurance about the straight dark brows, the clear-cut mouth, the broad shoulders under a faultlessly cut charcoal suit. Today he wore a grey tie patterned with tiny red diamonds, and his paler grey shirt was pristine. When he spooned half a teaspoon of sugar into his coffee she saw a gleaming cufflink in his sleeve, a tiny dark red stone set into one corner of an initialled gold square. Not many men of his age used cufflinks these days. His hands looked smooth but strong and masculine, and he wore no rings.

Although not spectacularly handsome, he had an indefinable low-key attraction. She wasn't surprised that Tansy had fallen for him. It had probably been all too easy for him to dazzle her, not least because a lecturer was someone she would naturally look up to.

He sat thoughtfully stirring the drink in front of him. When he leaned back and put down the spoon he asked abruptly, 'Just what did Tansy tell you about me?'

Was he anxious about his job? she wondered. It wouldn't look good for him to be known to have caused one of his students to attempt suicide. There'd been a time when Tansy had told her everything, but lately they had tacitly refrained from discussing him.

'Does it matter?' she asked. 'You needn't worry that I'm going to make trouble. For myself, I'd love to see you come thoroughly unstuck. But Tansy's welfare is my main concern, and I don't think she needs any more stress right now.'

'Is it any use telling you that I'm not responsible for what she did?'

'Legally, I'm sure you're in the clear. Morally——'

'Is she getting help?'

'Help?'

'Psychiatric help,' he said bluntly.

'It's good of you to be so concerned—at last,' Fler said. 'The hospital crisis team talked to her.'

'Crisis team?'

'Nurses who liaise with a psychiatrist, but they didn't feel it was necessary for her to see him.'

'No?' He was looking at her in a slightly bothered, undecided fashion. 'She's not normal, you know.'

Fler gave him a hostile stare. She'd seldom heard anything so ridiculous. Tansy wasn't the only girl in the world to over-react when her first love-affair went wrong. No one had suggested she was mentally ill. 'If you mean that she's mad to think that you are worth trying to kill herself over, I'd have to agree.'

She saw him quell a spurt of temper. He said levelly, 'It's not just that. She's been——' he spread his hands '—fantasising about things.'

'About you.'

'Well . . . yes.' He bent his head, almost as if embarrassed, and rubbed a hand briefly at the back of his neck. 'It's . . . a difficult situation,' he said.

'You mean, since you lost interest in her.'

'It wasn't quite like that,' he said less patiently. 'Whatever Tansy likes to think, there was never any great love-affair.'

'I see. Just a sordid little encounter or two, a bit of harmless fun?' Her voice was raw with resentment. It hurt to think he had taken so lightly what Tansy had so generously offered him.

'There was nothing sordid about it,' he said shortly.

Tansy certainly hadn't thought so. She'd thought it was the love-story of the century. 'And it wasn't harmless either,' Fler said swiftly, 'for Tansy.'

'Look,' he said, his eyes holding hers. 'For what it's worth, I suppose I handled it badly. I tried at first to let her down lightly. It didn't work. In the end maybe I was too—brutal. What you don't seem to understand is how unreasonable she was. I couldn't let it go on. And there was nothing in it. It was all totally one-sided.'

'Are you saying she imagined all of it?' This was unbelievable. 'That you never took her out, never touched her?'

He was silent for a moment. 'I went out with her,' he admitted. 'A couple of times. I didn't know then that she was a student,' he told her.

Fler allowed her brows to rise fractionally in disbelief, but said nothing.

He said, 'She looked all of twenty-five when we met. It was a party. We talked. I took her home. The point is——'

'The point is, you don't want anything more to do with her.' He was obviously bent on denying any real involvement, any culpability.

He hesitated only briefly. 'In a nutshell, yes. But I'd like you to understand——'

'I understand perfectly. You've been playing my daughter for months like a fish on a line. Now the game's suddenly turned serious and you want out! Your career might suffer if this story gets about. You even feel a little—just a little—guilty. Are you married?' It was a suspicion she'd entertained for some time, been afraid to voice to Tansy.

He looked startled at that, and angry. 'No, I'm not married! If I had been I'd never have gone near the girl in the first place.'

Fler let her scepticism show. His type didn't change their spots with marriage. He'd probably still be running after nubile students when he was in his dotage, and not able so easily to persuade them into falling in love with him.

'She's a nice young woman,' he said quietly. 'I liked her. But the whole thing got out of hand.' He shook his head. 'I think you ought to persuade her to have some kind of counselling.'

The nurses had suggested it, but when Tansy rejected the idea they hadn't really argued. The consensus seemed to be that she'd over-reacted and given everyone, including herself, a nasty fright, but that it was unlikely to be repeated.

'Would that salve your conscience, Mr Ranburn?' Fler asked him. 'It's easy for you, isn't it? Turn her over to other people to pick up the pieces, and find yourself some other poor little innocent whose life you can wreck.'

He leaned across the small table, the hazel eyes greening with temper. '*I have not wrecked anyone's life*!'

Ignoring the denial, Fler went on, her own temper rising, her skin heating and the nerve-ends prickling. 'Is Tansy the first one to go this far? Maybe I *should* talk to the university board about your activities with female students. People like you ought to be stopped before they do any permanent damage.'

'I've tried to explain,' he said tightly. 'But you don't want to listen——'

'Has it occurred to you,' she asked him, going much further than she had ever intended, 'that Tansy might be pregnant?'

She stopped abruptly there. Until she said it, she hadn't realised herself that it was a fear that had been lurking at the back of her mind.

She appeared to have stunned him, too. He stared at her for a second, then gave a harsh bark of laughter. 'If she is, she'd better not try to lay *that* at my door!'

Fler felt a hot thundering of pure fury in her head. But before it could explode into action, he'd pushed himself out of the booth and stood up. Looking down at her, he said, 'I don't think I've got through to you any more than I could to your daughter. But if you want a bit of advice, here it is. Because I'm just about at the end of my patience with her. *Get her off my back*!'

Watching his rapid progress to the door, Fler barely restrained herself from hurling her untouched cup of coffee after him.

# CHAPTER THREE

TANSY hadn't objected to Fler's plan to take her home. She didn't want to face her flatmates yet, she said shamefacedly. Would her mother go over there and pack up some of her clothes?

It was only two weeks to the August holidays. Maybe missing that fortnight wouldn't be too disastrous. If she didn't go back to university after the holidays, though, she'd have no chance of passing her first-year exams.

They'd have over a month to decide, Fler thought, looking through drawers in the flat and folding undies, shirts, jeans into a bag. She hesitated over the photograph of Tansy with her father and Fler, and decided to leave it.

'Need any help?' One of the flatmates peeked round the door. They'd been helpful, embarrassed, subdued when Fler arrived. And anxious about Tansy. That had warmed her, their genuine concern and shock at what had nearly happened. So different, she thought, from Kyle Ranburn's patent self-interest. 'We had no idea!' they'd told her, stricken at their own lack of awareness. 'Why did she want to do that?'

Fler hadn't told them why, respecting Tansy's agonised plea, 'Don't tell them! I feel such a fool.'

Fler smiled at the girl. 'I think I've found everything she's likely to need.'

'Don't forget her diary.'

Diary? Tansy had never kept a diary before. Fler looked about, and the girl came into the room and plucked a thick, hard-covered volume with a small gilt lock on it from among the books on a shelf over the bed. 'I think she'd want it. She nearly went spare once when she thought she'd lost it. We finally found it down the back of the sofa. She'd been writing it up in front of the TV. Forgot to take it back to her room. She must have been tired.'

'Thank you.' Fler tucked the book down into the front of the bag. 'Do you know where she keeps the key?'

The girl shook her head. 'Secret. I wouldn't be surprised if she's got it on a chain around her neck.'

There had been no chain around Tansy's neck. When she got to the hospital she'd been wearing her watch, a pair of panties and a night-shirt under the blanket that Kyle Ranburn had wrapped about her before bundling her into his car. 'I'll find it,' Fler said.

'Good luck, then.'

It wasn't in the musical box on the dressing-table, nor on any of the cluttered shelves. Knowing her daughter's habits, she eventually found the tiny brass key hanging on a nail inside the wardrobe. About to place it safely in her handbag, she paused, looking at the diary that it fitted. *No*, she said to herself firmly. Being Tansy's mother didn't give her the right to violate her privacy.

By the time the Toyota breasted the Brynderwyn hills and began the long descent towards the township of Waipu and the long stretch of road running by the sea at Ruakaka, Tansy was beginning to lose some of her extreme pallor.

They'd been travelling for over an hour and a half and she'd scarcely spoken two words, but now she stirred in her seat and said, 'It seems ages since I was home.'

It had been a weekend two months ago. Fler said, 'It seems a long time to me, too.'

In the blue distance the jagged uneven peaks of Manaia rose from the glitter of the sea. According to Maori legend the tall, commanding rocks standing stark against the sky at the summit were the petrified figures of the chief Manaia and his family. Lower and closer, the striped towers of the oil refinery at Marsden Point stood near the shore, an equally impressive modern echo.

Fler didn't stop at Whangarei, the small northern city cradled between bush-covered hills and a tranquil harbour, but continued north along the Tutukaka Coast road that wound through softly folded farmlands latticed with stone walls, and sometimes narrowed between stands of trees or to accommodate a short bridge over a shallow stream.

Then they were down near the sea again, driving alongside a sandy stretch of coastline, climbing once more before turning down the twisting road that led to Manaaki, the big old house overlooking the sea at Hurumoana. Glancing at Tansy, Fler was sure that the girl looked more relaxed already, her eyes brighter and her shoulders less hunched.

'Nearly home,' Fler said.

Oh, God, she prayed, let her be all right. Please let everything be all right.

Fortunately the guest house had few visitors at this time of the year. Most of the rooms were empty, and in the neighbouring bay the motor camp with its rows of cabins was almost deserted. The sea thundered into the gap between the rocks below the house, pulling at long strings of brown seaweed that looked like dark hair streaming in the water, and turning over the fine pebbly shingle below the crescent of white sand on the tiny enclosed beach. A salty winter wind flattened the *manuka* growing at the edge of the cliffs and set the brittle sword-leaved flax rattling and bending before it.

Tansy settled into her old room and spent the first few days listlessly sitting on the window seat facing the garden, gazing out through the glass, an unread book or her open diary in her lap. Sometimes she pulled on a jacket and went down the cliff path to the beach, scuffing among the small grey pebbles and broken shells along the strip of sand and then sitting on the rocks to watch the foam-flecked water hurtle by.

Fler would stand at the lounge window, her heart thudding, until Tansy got up and slowly made her way over the rocks to the sand again, to climb the path to the house.

'Don't you worry, she's not going to throw herself in the sea.' Rae Topia put a comforting brown hand on Fler's shoulder. She was the only full-time staff member that Fler kept on through the winter months, and over five years she'd become a friend as well as an employee.

Fler turned from her contemplation of the rocks and the raging water. Tansy was on her way up now, hidden by the steep drop of the cliff. 'I can't help worrying.'

Rae's brown eyes were sympathetic, her comfortable figure somehow reassuring in its motherly bulk. 'She'll come right. You wait.'

Within a few weeks it seemed that Rae's prediction was coming true. Tansy's appetite improved, her cheeks began to fill out a little and take on their normal soft-rose colour, and she even laughed sometimes. One night she came into Fler's room before her mother turned out the light, sat on the bed and said, 'Mum, I'm sorry I worried you like that. It was a dumb thing to do.'

'Yes, it was,' Fler told her frankly. 'Honestly, sweetheart, no man is worth it, believe me!'

Tansy shook her head. 'I s'pose not,' she said, looking down. 'I promise I'll never, ever do that again. But...I don't know how I can live without him!'

Fler's heart sank. She opened her arms, and Tansy threw herself into them and sobbed her heart out.

When Tansy said she was going to return to Auckland and her studies after the holiday, Fler was torn between fear and relief. The thought of Tansy dropping out of university was dismaying, but going back meant she'd be within Kyle Ranburn's orbit again. Was Tansy ready for that? His name hadn't been mentioned between them since that night she'd cried in her mother's arms.

But even if Tansy was still carrying a torch, he'd made it brutally clear that he was no longer interested. If he ever had been.

He'd said it was all one-sided on Tansy's part. Yet he'd admitted to taking her out 'a couple of times'. That was probably downplaying it. So it hadn't all been on Tansy's side at the beginning. Not for the first time, Fler felt a swift rush of impotent anger with the man who'd carelessly, selfishly almost ruined her daughter's life. Tansy, brought up in the north where life was slower and kinder and less sophisticated than in Auckland, must have been a pushover for an unscrupulous older man.

The night before Tansy was to leave again, Fler resisted the temptation to persuade her to stay or to extract impossible promises to phone every day, to let her mother know immediately of the slightest problem, to look after herself and please not pine after a worthless man who didn't want her anyway.

Instead, as they leaned side by side on the wide rail of the veranda, both dressed in jeans and woollens after a walk on the windblown beach, she looked out at the sunlight dying on the sea and said, 'Let me know if you need me, darling. You know I'll always come.'

Tansy turned and gave her a hug. 'I know,' she said. 'Thank you.'

Fler thought that was all she was going to say, but she leaned back against the rail and, with her head bent, said almost inaudibly, 'You think I'm an idiot, don't you?'

'Of course not!'

'Well, I s'pose I am,' Tansy muttered. 'But...you don't understand what it's like!'

Fler debated inwardly for a second. 'I have been in love, you know,' she said mildly.

'*Not like this*!'

The intensity of the statement startled Fler. But she supposed at eighteen she'd been equally intense, and just as convinced that no one else had ever felt as deeply as she did. Banishing a natural impatience at the arrogance of youth, she said, 'I suppose everyone's experience of love is unique. Especially first love.'

'Was Daddy your first love?'

'Well . . . yes.' The couple of crushes she'd had in early puberty didn't count.

'And you've never looked at anyone else since you broke up with him, have you?'

There hadn't been that many for her to look at, Fler thought, apart from the fact that she'd been rather soured on men and relationships after the divorce. She certainly hadn't been looking for a new mate. 'Not really,' she agreed cautiously.

Tansy moved again, turning with a hand on the post at the top of the steps, gazing at the first bright cold stars appearing between streaky winter clouds. 'Do you remember the first time you and Daddy kissed?' she asked dreamily.

'Yes, I do.' Her own voice softened. It was one of her better memories. Rick had been her only lover. She hadn't been aware then that not only was she not the first for him, but she wasn't to be the last, either. That kiss had melted her bones, brought her budding womanhood into full flower, made her aware of the power and pleasure of sex. Rick had been no novice, and he'd enjoyed teaching her.

Tansy said, 'I thought I'd *die*, the first time Kyle kissed me. I really thought...I'd die, it was so...wonderful.' She shivered—Fler saw it even under the bulky woollen sweater—and then wrapped her arms about herself. 'He was so gentle with me, always,' she murmured. 'Then and...and later. Of course, he knew I was a virgin, that's why.' She gave a little laugh. 'Men can tell, can't they? If they're...you know, experienced. I think it sort of frightened him, almost. Wasn't that sweet? I told him he didn't have to worry about it. It's not really a problem, these days.'

Fler firmly clamped her teeth together until her jaw ached. Her mouth felt dry. Her mind was filled with murder. 'Did he——' her voice sounded hoarse '—hurt you?'

'No.' Tansy turned round to face her, but in the dusky gloom cast by the shadow of the veranda her face was just a pale blur. 'Have I shocked you?'

'I'm not shocked.' A lie. She felt as though someone had punched her in the stomach. 'I've always said, there's nothing you can't tell me, Tansy. If you want to.' She took a deep, quick breath and asked, 'Darling, you're not pregnant, are you?'

For a moment she almost thought she'd shocked Tansy. There was a silence, finally broken by a blessed, normal, youthful, astonished laugh, like the old Tansy who'd had not a care in the world. 'Oh, Mum!' she said, giving Fler another quick hug. 'Is that what you've been worrying about? No, I'm not. Definitely. And there's no danger, I promise. I do know how to take care of myself.'

Fler bit back a retort. She didn't want to start sounding old and fussy and change Tansy's confiding mood.

But apparently the confidences were over, anyway. Tansy shivered again, with cold this time, and said, 'Let's go in. I need an early night.'

'I'll have to get down to Auckland more often,' Fler said, sharing a cup of tea in the big kitchen with Rae after putting Tansy on the bus in Whangarei. 'I'm so afraid for her. It's going to take her some time to get over that wretched man. Maybe I should have moved when she started at university. Bought a place in Auckland so she could live at home. She's so young to be on her own.'

'You went over all that last year,' Rae reminded her. 'What happened to letting her find her feet, spreading her wings, leaving the nest, et cetera?'

Fler laughed. 'Did I really inflict all those clichés on you?'

Rae patted her hand. 'You were right when you said those things. Sure she'll make mistakes, and get her heart broken once or twice. And of course you'll cry for her. But we can't keep our kids from being hurt forever. Like when they were little and learning to walk, we didn't hold their hands every minute, just picked them up when they fell over and gave them a kiss.'

'Yes.' Fler smiled. Rae was right. She'd made the decision not to move for just those reasons. Being a solo mother with an only child, she'd been aware of the danger of stifling Tansy's independence. She had to learn to let go, yet be there when she was needed. It was a difficult balancing act.

'By the way,' Rae told her, changing the subject, 'the University Extension people phoned while you were out, to confirm their dates for the summer school next year. I've put them in the book.'

'Oh, good.' With a deliberate effort, Fler wrenched her mind around to business. For the past few years the university in conjunction with local groups had run a three-week summer school from the end of January into February, based at Hurumoana.

Some tutors were local, but others from the university staff stayed at the guest house, and the motor camp just five minutes' walk away accommodated many of the students. It meant the guest house was fully booked when the peak holiday season was just declining.

It wasn't always easy to get to Auckland but Fler made sure she visited Tansy several times in the following months. To her relief, the girl seemed to be working hard—too hard? Fler wondered anxiously, noting her thinness and hollow eyes.

When Fler tentatively asked if she had seen Kyle Ranburn, Tansy gave her a rather peculiar look and said, 'I'm in his class on social factors in nineteenth-century New Zealand. Of course I *see* him. But I don't embarrass him. I know he'd hate that.'

'Well, good,' Fler murmured rather uncertainly. It galled her that Tansy was still more concerned about that unscrupulous exploitative male than about her own feelings. But clearly she would brook no criticism of her idol.

Tansy said, 'I had a talk with Kyle. He was very understanding. Those pills, you know... it was just a way of getting attention. Nothing like that will happen again. From now on I'm going to be an adult.'

Fler didn't know whether to laugh or cry. But she supposed that was good news. She hoped Tansy was able to live up to her resolution.

Exam time came and then Tansy was home for the long Christmas holidays. She looked tired and pale and slept a lot the first few days, but said it was just the stress of examinations. She helped out around the guest house when the usual holiday influx arrived and, as she had for the last few years, Fler put her on the payroll.

'But I can't stay through until February,' Tansy told her. 'I've put my name down for an archaeology dig in the South Island. Someone found a pioneer village buried in the bush down there, from the days of the Otago gold rush. They need students to help, and it'd be good for my course credits.'

Swallowing disappointment, Fler said, 'It sounds fun. Will they pay you?'

'Uh-uh. But it's experience. And...well, I want to go. You don't mind, do you?'

Of course she didn't mind, Fler assured her. 'If you need some money for expenses, I could help out with a small loan.'

'Thanks.' Tansy gave her a quick kiss on the cheek. 'My courses are costing you enough as it is. I'll try to do without a subsidy for this.'

She didn't mention Kyle Ranburn all the time she was home, and Fler thought, That must be all over, thank goodness. When Fler saw her off in time for the South Island trip, Tansy looked almost glowing with anticipation.

'Will you miss me?' she teased as Fler kissed her goodbye.

'Of course I will.' Fler smiled back at her and touched a fingertip to her nose as she used to when Tansy was a little girl. 'You behave, now.'

Tansy laughed as she clambered aboard the bus lugging a bulging red pack. It was good to see her so happy, Fler thought. Quite her old self again.

The next week was a busy period for the guest house. As visitors moved out the rooms had to be prepared for those shortly moving in. The local organiser of the summer school who liaised with the university course co-ordinator was continually checking on this detail or that.

Rae and Fler allotted rooms for the tutors and the course co-ordinator. There was to be a creative writing course and one on European influences in the Pacific, as well as a geology group, print-making, a marine biology class and a course in video filming, all taught by visiting tutors from the university. Advanced pottery and two art classes were being conducted by local and visiting artists, and a saturation course in spoken Maori was to be centred on the nearby *marae*.

The course co-ordinator, a smartly dressed young woman with an air of brisk efficiency, arrived driving a van full of assorted teaching materials. She was followed within minutes by four of the tutors sharing a car. Fler was ushering the co-ordinator into her room while Rae did the same for the others, when they heard another car draw up in the courtyard outside.

The young woman peered out the window and said, 'That'll be the other tutor arriving now. Oh, by the way, you'll have Mr Hathaway down for a room, but unfortunately he couldn't make it after all. He made sure we got a very good replacement for European influences in the Pacific, though. It won't make any difference to you, anyway, will it?'

'None at all,' Fler assured her, as the bell at the reception desk rang. 'If you have everything you need...?'

'I'm fine.' The young woman put a bag on the bed and looked about. 'I'm dying to use the loo, though. Will you tell him, please, that we're all going to meet in the lounge in half an hour?'

'Yes, I will. There's a coffee machine there. I'll make sure it's refilled before then.'

'That would be lovely. Thanks.'

The bell pealed again. Along the hall, Rae was still talking to one of the tutors who was asking where the nearest pub was.

Fler made for the stairs, and turned at the bottom to cross to the desk at one side of the entrance hall.

The man who had been lounging against the counter, idly studying one of the guest house's address cards that he'd picked up from there, turned to face her as she approached. For a moment his expression was blank, then his hazel eyes suddenly darkened with shock and he straightened abruptly. 'I don't believe it!' he said in stunned tones. 'What in *hell* are you doing here?'

# CHAPTER FOUR

FLER blinked. She felt pretty much the same way, herself. 'I'm the proprietor,' she said. 'If you're looking for Tansy, Mr Ranburn, she isn't here.' It gave her some satisfaction to be able to tell him that. Tansy might have been pleased to think of him coming after her, but Fler was convinced this man was nothing but bad news for her daughter.

'Tansy?' he said blankly, as though he'd forgotten who that was, and Fler immediately wanted to hit him. She'd like nothing more than for him to stay well away from Tansy, but he didn't have to make it so obvious that he didn't really give a damn.

Before she could say anything he glanced again at the card in his hand. '"F.H. Daniels, proprietor",' he read aloud. 'I thought you were Mrs Hewson.'

'I answer to my ex-husband's name sometimes,' she told him. 'Especially in matters concerning Tansy. It saves explanations.'

He was still looking at her as though hoping she was going to disappear in a puff of smoke. The feeling was mutual, she wanted to assure him. Instead she said crisply, with only the forlornest hope that it wasn't true, 'If you're not here to see Tansy, I presume you're one of the tutors for the summer school. The others arrived ten minutes ago.'

'Well, good,' he said absently, looking as though he was trying to think of an excuse to leave. She wished he would.

'Do you need any help with bags?' she asked him.

'Ah...no. No, I'll manage. Thank you,' he added, belatedly. 'Tansy——'

'She's in the South Island,' she told him. 'Until the end of February. If you're ready, I'll take you to your room. You can sign the book later.'

She didn't want to discuss Tansy with him. Didn't want to discuss anything with him. Didn't know how she was going to bear being in the same house with the man for the next three weeks. But she could hardly throw him out without explanation, and explanations would be humiliating for Tansy. The story would be bound to get back to the university.

'This way,' she said coldly, and led him up the stairs.

The only bright spot, Fler told herself later, filling the coffee machine, checking the sugar bowls and placing milk and cream on the lace-covered table, was that Tansy *wasn't* here. At least she'd have had a three-month respite from his pernicious influence before she saw Kyle Ranburn again.

She opened up the wide doors that let in the sea breeze, and plumped some of the pastel-patterned cushions on the cane sofas and chairs around the room. It was quite hot. Iced water might be preferred by some of the guests to coffee.

She went to the kitchen to fill a jug, and also fetched a packet of biscuits and a plate. Perhaps it was the crackle of the packet as she opened it, pouring the biscuits expertly in overlapping circles on to the plate, that prevented her from hearing Kyle Ranburn come into the room.

When she turned and found him beside her, she jumped.

'Sorry,' he said. He'd been reaching for a cup, but now he stepped back. 'I didn't mean to startle you.' He was staring a little, but she supposed she was too. He looked different, from when they'd first met at the hospital. It was probably the casual clothes he wore, jeans and a denim bomber-style jacket over a dark T-shirt.

What the well-dressed lecturer wears when catering to the country masses, she thought nastily. This man would look good in anything. He actually looked sexier now than in the suit she'd seen him in before.

Dismissing the thought, she turned away from him, but looked back when he said abruptly, 'You're alike, aren't you—you and your daughter?'

'*What*?' Could he have picked up that wayward thought? Her eyes sparked with chagrin.

'Hasn't anyone commented on it before? For a second, as I came in, I thought you were her.'

'Oh.' Fool, of course he hadn't meant *that*! Fler swallowed. 'Yes, actually they have.' Her voice sounded stiff, reluctant. She made to walk round him, get out of the room. No one else had come down yet.

Surprisingly, he caught at her arm as she went to pass him, not hard but firmly. 'Just a minute!'

Fler pulled away from him almost violently. 'Don't you touch me!' All her nerve-ends were tingling, the fine hairs on her skin prickling up with antagonism.

'I'm not going to assault you,' he said shortly, looking thoroughly fed up. Also rather disconcerted, as though he'd just suffered a small shock. 'I only wanted to say...' He stopped to frame the words.

'Say what?'

'It looks as though we're stuck with each other for several weeks. If I'd known—but I didn't, and it's too late now for me to back out. I wouldn't want the others to——'

Contempt for him almost choked her. But she said, 'Don't worry, Mr Ranburn. I'm not likely to start telling all and sundry my daughter's private business. You're quite safe.'

He closed his eyes momentarily, saying something under his breath, then opened them again. They were like a wintry sea, a deep anger in them. 'Look, I——'

He was interrupted by the course co-ordinator coming into the room. 'Mr Ranburn?' she said, advancing with her hand held out as he turned to her. 'I'm Devina Roache. I don't believe we've met.'

Her eyes discreetly signalled that she was awfully glad to remedy that. She was tall, and her sleek dark hair framed a smooth-skinned, perfectly oval face that had everything in the right places, as did her figure, shown off by a brief skirt and even briefer top that she'd changed into.

Fler didn't fail to notice the flicker of appreciation in Kyle Ranburn's eyes as he clasped the proffered hand in his. Obviously not one to miss any opportunity, she thought. She thanked God again that Tansy wasn't here to be hurt all over again. And was suddenly conscious of being on the wrong side of thirty-five, and that the comfortable cotton trousers and big shirt which she'd considered perfectly suitable this morning for the casual, relaxed atmosphere that the guests enjoyed were neither smart nor particularly feminine.

They hardly noticed, she was persuaded, when she muttered an excuse and left them to it. The other tutors were coming down the stairs now, talking companionably. One of the men smiled at her absently as they swept into the lounge.

He was tall with curly dark hair and blue eyes, and objectively was better looking than Kyle Ranburn. But he didn't have that indefinable aura the other man had, the pull of attraction that had brought that inviting light

to Devina Roache's eyes, that had seduced poor Tansy.
And——

Fler crossed the empty dining-room and viciously
pushed open the saloon-type doors to the kitchen. Cut
that out! she told herself. The man's an unscrupulous
opportunist. A sexual gourmet in the same mould as
Rick Hewson. Worse. He preyed on girls who held him
in awe because he was their teacher.

In the dining-room that evening the long table was the
centre of happy chatter and a good deal of laughter.
Manaaki wasn't licensed, but some of the guests brought
their own wine to the table, and the atmosphere was
relaxed.

As usual they were a friendly lot. A couple of them
had been involved in the summer schools before. They
joked with the young Maori waitresses and chatted to
Fler who supervised and unobtrusively helped to serve
when it was needed. She noticed that Devina Roache
was seated next to Kyle Ranburn, but although the young
woman was sparkling he appeared slightly preoccupied,
smiling absentmindedly rather than joining in the
laughter about him.

After dinner they spent an hour or so in the lounge
discussing their programme, and some lingered on,
helping themselves to coffee. It was quite late when Fler,
finding the room empty at last, stacked the dirty cups
on to a tray and crossed the room to close the glass doors
before carrying the dishes to the kitchen.

A man standing on the veranda outside turned from
his contemplation of the night and the intermittent
moonlit ripples on the sea. It was dark and she couldn't
see his face.

Pausing with her hand on the door she'd been about
to close, she said, 'I'm just about to lock up, but if you

don't want to come in yet, would you put the latch up when you do?'

'I'm coming in now.'

She recognised the voice and, when he came into the light, his face.

He walked past her and waited while she shot the bolts home. 'Devina says this room is to be my classroom,' he said.

'Oh?' She hadn't taken much notice of the programme; the co-ordinators arranged all that. Messy activities were usually planned for the community hall, while those comprising mainly lectures were reserved for the guest house.

'I'm told,' he went on, 'that you're very co-operative, very helpful.'

'I try to be.'

'I wondered if I might have a table in my room. It doesn't need to be very big.'

There was a long built-in desk-cum-dressing-table, but it wasn't the first time a tutor had requested something wider. 'Would a card table do?'

'Yes. Fine. Provided it's reasonably stable.'

Crisply she said, 'I'll see to it. Anything else?'

He seemed to be hesitating. 'No,' he said finally. 'Except——'

She didn't help him out. She had a fair idea that he was going to try yet again to justify himself.

He spoke slowly. 'These summer schools are special. Everyone says there's an atmosphere about them that they don't experience anywhere else. Your—hospitality and friendliness, and your staff's, apparently have quite a lot to do with that.'

'Thank you.' From anyone else she'd have accepted the accolade with pleasure. Now she just wondered what he was leading up to.

He gave a sharp sigh. 'What I'm trying to say is, it would be a pity to spoil that. Do you think that for the next three weeks you could try to forget how much you hate me? For everyone's sake.'

She didn't think that anyone else had noticed. She'd not spoken to him at dinner, but then he'd scarcely looked directly at her either. And they wouldn't have thought anything of it. He wasn't one of those who'd been here before.

She said, 'I've been running this place for five years, Mr Ranburn. My staff and I are used to being polite to obnoxious guests—not, fortunately, that we've had very many. We never allow a personal dislike of anyone to affect the level of service they're given.'

He stirred irritably. 'That wasn't quite what I meant, and I'm sure you know it. I don't think I've ever met anyone with your ability to somehow tackle an issue side-on.'

'I really don't know what you're talking about.'

'You know damn well, you infuriating woman!'

Fler said coolly, 'We're also accustomed to dealing with rudeness. But that doesn't mean we just lie down and take it.'

'Is this a royal we?' he enquired.

Sarcastic brute. 'I thought you were asking me to be nice to you,' she suggested. 'If you expect that while you feel free to insult me——'

'It wasn't meant to be insulting.' As she pointedly refrained from comment, he added, 'But all right, I apologise for losing my temper. Believe it or not, it doesn't happen often.'

No, he was a cold-blooded animal. She angered him because she had seen through him from the start, Fler decided. 'Apology accepted,' she said. 'And you needn't worry that my real opinion of you will be in any way apparent to your colleagues, Mr Ranburn.' She would be the epitome of politeness and co-operation; he'd have absolutely nothing to fault her for. But he needn't expect friendliness. That would be asking the impossible.

He said very formally, with just a hint of irony, 'Thank you. Perhaps you could start by calling me Kyle. I noticed that you're on first-name terms with everyone else, even those who are here for the first time like me.'

Of course she was. There was never any formality at Manaaki, particularly during the summer school. 'Yes,' she said. 'All right.'

'Good.' He stood for a while facing her as though undecided about something. Then he said deliberately, 'Goodnight, Fler.'

No one had said her name quite as this man did, lingering over the single syllable as if he could taste it on his tongue, his voice deep and slow. An odd sensation passed over her skin, warm and feathery, as if he had physically touched her.

She shook herself mentally, and clenched her fists against an involuntary shiver.

He was waiting, looking at her. She hoped her eyes weren't giving away the sudden agitated thumping of her heart. She moistened her lower lip and kept her voice flat, indifferent. 'Goodnight—Kyle.'

She picked up the tray and took it out, her hands perfectly steady, her mind filled with dismay.

Packing the cups and saucers into the dishwasher in the kitchen, she tried to rationalise.

He had something, undoubtedly, some kind of sex appeal that wasn't immediately apparent, not all on the surface, and the more potent for that. The man was an expert manipulator, she reminded herself, obviously with a lot of practice. He knew perfectly well what effect he had on women, and OK, she wasn't immune.

But she was no adolescent innocent, ready to fall at his feet because he said her name in a way that made it sound special. She was a grown woman—older than him, for heaven's sake! Even if she hadn't been wise to his games, she had no reason to suppose he'd have been interested in her! His taste ran to younger women. Much younger. Although Devina Roache, for all the unlined perfection of her features, must be over twenty-five.

Not as much over as you are, a mean-spirited inner voice jeered. You're the *mother* of one his conquests! He wouldn't look twice in your direction.

Stop there! Fler ordered herself, appalled at the trend of her thoughts.

Of course she didn't want to catch Kyle Ranburn's eye. The less she had to do with him the better. The summer school this year couldn't be over and done with soon enough for her.

But it hadn't even started, yet.

Next morning eager students of all ages from teenagers to white-haired eighty-year-olds descended on the tiny beach community and were speedily dispatched to makeshift classrooms, all within convenient walking distance of the community hall. By ten o'clock, cars had stopped arriving and relative quiet reigned as everyone settled in for the first sessions.

Fler ushered an apologetic late-comer into the front lounge, and returned to the desk to do some bookwork. The door to the lounge was open to allow a cooling breeze to circulate, and she could clearly hear Kyle launching into his session. He would be accustomed to addressing a lecture hall full of students, of course. Although, didn't they use microphones these days? Anyway, he had a good, deep, clear voice, easy to listen to...

Finding that was what she was doing, she bent her head to the books.

A burst of laughter came from the lounge. Tansy had said he often made his students laugh, it was one of the things she liked about his classes. 'With him it all comes alive,' she had said eagerly. 'He makes the people seem real, not just words in history books.'

Fler picked up a ruler and drew a precise red line under a set of figures. Tansy had said he was brilliant at his subject. But then, she might have been biased.

At lunchtime Fler helped the kitchen staff serve salad, fruit and cheese for the lecturers. The students either brought their own lunch or made other arrangements.

Kyle said to her, 'Do you mind if I take mine outside?' Some of the students were picnicking on the lawn or the veranda steps.

'Whatever you like,' Fler told him. 'Just return the plate later.'

He brought it back as Fler was clearing away the cheese. 'Sorry, I got talking.'

Fler reluctantly asked, 'Would you like some cheese?'

'Thanks.' Casually he picked a chunk off the plate she was holding.

'What about coffee?'

He smiled at her. 'You do live up to your reputation, don't you?'

'I'm doing my best.'

The smile turned wry. 'You know, I'm *not* the big bad wolf, and I didn't gobble up your Little Red Riding Hood.'

'"But Grandma, what big teeth you have"!' Fler said.

He laughed, then. He didn't have particularly big teeth, but they were white and even. He looked down at her, the laughter still in his eyes, making him look—damn him!—more dangerously attractive than ever.

Fler swallowed, clamping her own teeth together to stop an involuntary smile.

Kyle shook his head, put the chunk of cheese in his mouth and sauntered out.

# CHAPTER FIVE

FLER picked her way across the drift of pebbles and shells and walked into the gentle breakers, wading up to her thighs before plunging under the cool water.

Visitors were told they should take the short walk across the headland to the longer, sandier and gentler beach next door. But on hot summer evenings like this the sea washing into the little cove was tranquil, almost smooth, and a swim was a welcome refresher after a day's work in the heat.

It felt cold at first but soon warmed, and she stayed in until the last of the daylight was almost gone from the sky.

When she came out, she was surprised to see Kyle Ranburn sitting on the dry sand where she'd left her towel. He had changed into shorts and his feet were bare.

As she approached he got up and picked up her towel, shaking out the sand before handing it to her.

'Thanks,' she said rather curtly. He hadn't been waiting for her, had he? She'd probably been unrecognisable while in the water. Perhaps he'd hoped that it was one of the younger and more attractive female students.

'I thought this beach was unsafe for swimming?' he said.

'It's all right when it's calm, and provided you know where the rocks are. But the other beach is patrolled and better for visitors. We wouldn't like to be responsible for anyone getting into trouble in the water.'

'Mmm.' He was regarding her idly as she dried her hair and face, then blotted the towel over her shoulders and arms. 'How old *were* you when you had Tansy?'

Her head went up. 'What?'

He spread his hands. 'You look too young to be her mother. You must have been a child bride.'

'It's dark,' she reminded him. Twilight, anyway. Flippantly she sang a snatch of Gilbert and Sullivan. '"She may very well pass for forty-three in the dusk with a light behind her".'

He threw back his head and laughed. 'Are you forty-three?' he enquired.

'No, I'm not!' she said, ridiculously outraged. 'I was nineteen when Tansy was born.' She wound the towel about her waist and tucked the end in. That kind of flattery, she told herself firmly, was so obvious it was laughable. So what if he sounded perfectly sincere? No doubt it came easily with practice.

She thrust back her damp hair with one hand, and started towards the cliff path.

Kyle kept pace with her. 'How old were you when you got married, then?'

She cast him a frosty glance. 'Eighteen, and for the record it was eleven months before Tansy appeared on the scene.'

'I wasn't counting.'

She didn't answer that, and as they reached the path he said, 'You're only seven years older than me.'

'Congratulations,' she said. 'I thought your subject was history.'

He laughed again, briefly. 'Were you always this sassy?'

Sassy. It sounded American. Had he spent time in the States? 'It comes with age,' she said, going ahead of him up the steep path. 'I suppose your adoring young students wouldn't dare try to cut you down to size.'

'Most of them don't adore me,' he said.

'Just Tansy? Surely she's not the only one.'

He was silent until she had breasted the top of the cliff. She stamped out a small surge of disappointment. There was something about sparring with him that had sent a surge of adrenalin through her. She'd almost begun to enjoy herself.

She'd climbed too fast, and as she stopped at the top of the path to get her breath, he joined her on the coarse, springy buffalo grass. He said, 'Do you think we could make a pact?'

Wary again, she said, 'What kind of pact?'

'You've made up your mind about me, as far as your daughter is concerned. Whatever I say you're going to hold it against me. We've agreed not to spoil the summer school for everyone else by airing our—differences in public. But it's going to be difficult if every time we happen to bump into each other we come back to the subject.'

'Believe me, I'm doing my best not to bump into you, Mr Ranburn.'

'Kyle!'

Fler shrugged. 'Kyle.'

'We can't avoid each other forever,' he said. 'And I'm not sure I want to.'

Stupid, *stupid* to feel that involuntary lifting of the heart, the swift kick of pleasure. 'Very prettily put,' she said sarcastically. 'I'm sorry I can't say it's mutual. What exactly are you suggesting?'

'Nothing that would give you an excuse to slap my face,' he assured her drily. 'Not that I think you'd need an excuse, if you got half the chance. I just thought we might agree that while I'm here you and I don't discuss

Tansy at all. In fact, I suggest it's the only way we're going to manage to be reasonably civilised with each other for three weeks. Not to mention that I—well, anyway... how about it?'

He was making a lot of sense. It was true that it wasn't going to be possible to avoid each other completely. And if the bone of contention was made a taboo subject, it ought to help defuse the situation.

'All right,' Fler said. 'I agree.'

'Thank goodness for that.' He held out his hand, and after a moment's hesitation she put hers into it.

His fingers were strong and warm, his clasp firm but not too tight. And when she hastily withdrew her hand, startled at the pleasurable feel of his, he immediately let her go.

'You're cold,' he said. 'You'd better go in.'

She didn't feel cold. Her hand must have felt chilly to him after her swim. Obviously he hadn't experienced any pleasure from her touch. But she said, 'Yes, I will.' And left him standing on the edge of the cliff, looking after her.

Their bargain did make things less strained. True to her promise, Fler was careful not to treat him in any markedly different way from the others. He seemed to find it easy to adopt a casually friendly attitude towards her. And there were times when she realised to her astonishment that she had actually forgotten what he was, what he had done to her only child.

She would pull herself up with a jerk, then. And quietly, imperceptibly withdraw a little.

Except perhaps it wasn't quite imperceptible. Because Kyle gave her a quizzical look or two, and once a silent, chiding shake of the head, his lips pursed in mock censure.

\*       \*       \*

Each session of the summer school ran for two hours in the morning and two in the afternoon. That left ample time for socialising and for those staying at the bay to enjoy the beaches and go boating, windsurfing or surfboarding.

On Saturday some decided to visit the nearest licensed premises for a meal and to spend the evening, and another group opted for a barbecue on the beach.

Fler and her staff were invited to join them. After serving dinner at the guest house Fler sent the others off early and stayed behind to finish up. Rae had volunteered to return to Manaaki after going home for her own dinner, and Fler had a short, cooling swim, then walked over the headland in the slowly falling dusk to the bigger bay.

The crowd was gathered about a glowing fire, browning sausages and toasting marshmallows. The tall dark art tutor, Conrad Duncan, had almost insisted that she come, and when she arrived he hailed her with a pleased smile and with a friendly hand at her waist drew her into the crowd.

He introduced her to some of the students, and it wasn't until she felt a familiar prickling sensation, a shiver of awareness, that she realised Kyle was sitting on the other side of the fire. Devina Roache, casually yet immaculately dressed in a bulky sweater and white trousers, was leaning against his shoulder.

She smiled at Fler, and flipped a hand in greeting, but Kyle didn't smile, just gave her a rather penetrating look and a curt nod.

Fler raised her brows and pursed her lips in a parody of his own expression when he thought she was reneging on their bargain, and after a moment he laughed, making Devina turn a surprised stare on him.

Conrad urged Fler to a space near the fire, and a couple of people obligingly moved over so that they could both sit down.

Someone offered her a can of beer, and she took it with a murmur of thanks. Conrad leaned over and rescued a sausage on a skewer for her from several that were spitting fat into the fire. A packet of sliced bread materialised from somewhere and she dug out a piece to wrap the sausage in. Conrad found some tomato sauce, and they laughed as he managed to pour it on to her wrist as well as the sausage, so that she had to lick it away.

She recognised a plump woman on her other side as one of Kyle's history students. Politely, she asked the woman how she was enjoying the summer school.

'It's wonderful! I haven't had anything like this since my kids came along. They've all left home now and I'm just beginning to do some of the things I've always wanted to.'

Fler smiled at her. It was a story she'd heard over and over from women who came to the school. Some confessed to a yen to paint, or write, or take up some other long-abandoned interest that they had suppressed for the sake of their families. Others had been quite happy in their housewife-mother role until at forty-five, fifty, sixty, they found themselves redundant, and were casting about for something to give their lives meaning again. Now and then one would find through the school some unsuspected talent, develop a previously hidden ambition.

'Why history?' Fler asked, keeping her eyes on her neighbour, determined not to glance across the lowering flames to where Kyle sat. She wished this woman had taken another of the courses.

'I was good at history at school,' the woman told her. 'And I've always enjoyed historical novels. To tell you the truth, I was disappointed there was no European history course being offered this year, but Kyle has opened up a whole new world to me. He's a great teacher.'

'Really?'

'Mmm. And they say he's a ring-in, too. Pacific history's not his specialty.'

'He teaches a nineteenth-century New Zealand course at the university,' Fler told her. 'I suppose it's closely connected.'

'You know him well?'

Hastily, Fler disclaimed that. 'No, not at all. My daughter took one of his courses last year.'

'Lucky girl.'

Hardly. Fler felt a stirring of the bitter rage she'd been repressing. Involuntarily she turned her gaze to Kyle, and found him looking directly at her.

A frown appeared between his brows, and he leaned forward almost as though he would have spoken to her. But before he could, she had turned away.

There were many more women in the group than men. That was usual for all the courses. Some of the younger ones had left families with their husbands or friends. This generation were not so willing to wait for their children to leave home before they did something for themselves. 'I have to talk with real, grown-up people now and then,' one of them said, laughing. 'Otherwise I'd go mad and start chopping up my kids with a meat cleaver.'

One elderly man had worked all his life as a shop assistant. 'Now that I'm retired I want to keep the old grey cells active,' he told Fler. 'I left school at fourteen—my people couldn't afford to send me to university. I thought

I'd try this out. Next year I might enrol for some extra-mural courses. Kyle reckons there's no reason I shouldn't be able to get a degree, at my time of life.'

Kyle again. Fler sighed inwardly and turned back to Conrad. At least he didn't talk about Kyle. He had a lot to say about the merits and drawbacks of gouache and tempera and acrylics and other techniques that Fler had only vaguely heard of but tried valiantly to take an interest in.

The food was soon eaten, and a girl with a guitar led a sing-song. Later, there was a general stirring and several people got up and began shedding clothes for a swim.

'Going in?' Conrad asked Fler, pulling off his shirt.

'Not just now, thanks. I had a quick dip earlier, before I came down.'

Devina had taken off her sweater and trousers to reveal a sleek yellow swimsuit, cut low at the back and very high on her firm, shapely thighs. You had to be young and have a superb figure to look good in that, Fler reflected. Devina looked great.

She stood up herself, and Conrad said, 'Change your mind?'

Fler shook her head. 'I think I'll be getting home. Thanks, Conrad, it was fun. But I've got an early start in the morning. See you tomorrow.'

She walked away from the fire into darkness, hesitating as she waited for her eyes to adjust. But she knew the way well, and there was a summer moon.

She was climbing the shallow plant-netted dunes towards the path when she heard footfalls behind her and a torchlight danced over the dry, whippy *pingao* beach-grass ahead.

She turned, and Kyle's voice said, 'Did I startle you?'

'Not really. I thought you were swimming.'

'No. I've never been particularly fond of swimming in the dark. You didn't bring a torch. I thought I'd walk you home.'

'What about Devina?'

'Devina? What about her?' he echoed.

'Well . . . isn't she with you?'

'Not in the sense I think you mean. We came over in a group.'

Fler didn't think Devina would be pleased that he'd sloped off without her, all the same. She stopped herself from saying so. His ego didn't need any stroking. 'I know the path well,' she said. 'And I'm a big girl, quite capable of walking home on my own.'

'So is Devina,' he said. 'And she'll have plenty of others to walk with.' He paused. 'I've had enough of the party anyway. I've some preparation to do for Monday's lecture that I'd like to get over with tonight so I can have a day off tomorrow. But if you can't stand my company for the next five minutes, you'd better say so. I promise I'll retire in good order.'

There was a small pause, and he gave a harsh breath of laughter and said, 'I see. Sorry.' He made to go back the way he'd come.

Ashamed of her bad manners, Fler heard herself say, 'Kyle!'

As he turned enquiringly she said, '*I'm* sorry. It was kind of you to bother, and I'd . . . appreciate your company. Thank you.'

For a moment she thought he wasn't going to accept the apology. Then he seemed to relax. 'Thank *you*. That was graciously put.'

He moved forward and briefly touched her arm, then directed the torch beam to the ground in front of their feet.

The sandy path was bordered by sparse grasses and low, twisted coastal bushes. They passed a tall clump of *toe-toe* with sharp-edged, gracefully drooping leaves, surrounding stiffly-held pale plumes shivering in the night breeze off the sea. A desultory cricket chirruped from the windblown crinkly *akeake*, and the relentless hush and shush and occasional whoomph-thump of the waves echoed up the cliff.

The sky tonight was cloudless, and the stars were a dense shower of brilliance prodigally flung across the sky. As Fler and Kyle reached the top of the slope the moon brushed a silver sheen over the ruffled sea. From here the view was wide, a limitless expanse disappearing into the dark forever. It brought them to an admiring halt and kept them silent and enchanted for several minutes.

The sound of the sea from here deepened to a muted thundering where it flowed over the rocks and raced into the gap. The scent of it, sharp and pleasant, came to them where they stood, and a hint of cool, fine spray was on the air.

After a while Kyle said quietly, 'I suppose you're accustomed to this.'

'That doesn't make it any less awesome,' she murmured. 'And there are not many nights as beautiful as this.'

When at last they moved on, Fler was reluctant to speak again, and sensed that he was, too. For a little time they'd shared one of life's moments of timeless yet transient perfection. Neither of them wanted to mar it.

When they reached the broad veranda with the outside light attracting a covey of narrow moths, Kyle switched off the torch and moved ahead of her to open the big old-fashioned door into the empty lobby.

She passed him and said, 'Thank you. And for seeing me home.'

'Even though it was unnecessary?'

Fler shrugged, smiling. Some residue of the spell of the night was still on her. She was full of well-being, of a lingering strange delight.

'Goodnight,' she said. She should have turned away then, gone away and left him. But something in his eyes seemed to hold her there, unable to move.

'Goodnight, Fler.' And again she noticed the way he said her name, making something soft and vibrant uncurl within her.

She felt her lips part involuntarily, and saw his eyes watching, saw something flicker in them, some hunger that she recognised.

She recognised the same hunger in herself. It was years since she'd experienced it with such aching urgency.

Deliberately, she sank her teeth into her lower lip and made herself move back from him, drag her gaze away, turn to leave him.

He stepped forward swiftly, and she felt his strong hand curved about her wrist, pulling her round again to face him.

He was too close now. She looked up into his eyes fleetingly, then away. Agitatedly, she said, 'Let me go, Kyle, please. Please don't spoil it.'

He held her a moment longer and then reluctantly released his grip. She knew he was staring at her, but she didn't dare meet his eyes again. The light in them was too tempting, too potent. She was breathing fast, hurriedly. She shook her head. 'Goodnight,' she whispered again, and made herself turn her back on him, walking away so fast she was almost running.

# CHAPTER SIX

ON SUNDAY there were no classes. Breakfast was later than usual, but Fler managed to slip away afterwards to attend church in the small white-painted wooden building a couple of miles from the guest house while Rae covered for her.

She felt in need of some spiritual strength, disturbed by her reactions last night to a look, a fleeting touch, to a few minutes on a moonswept clifftop with a man.

A man, she reminded herself ruthlessly, who was seven years her junior, and who had been romantically involved with her own daughter. Nausea clutched at her stomach. She sat with the rest of the congregation and tried to concentrate on the sermon, but only a stray word penetrated now and then, her mind busily going about its own frenetic business.

Flattery, that was all it was. She'd been flattered that a younger, undeniably personable man could look at her with desire in his eyes. It was natural for a woman staring forty in the face to feel some pleasure in that. And because she'd been starved of any close male companionship for five years, she was particularly susceptible.

Starved. It wasn't a lack she'd been specially bothered by, most of the time. Why this sudden longing, this desperate emptiness and aloneness, now?

Because she no longer had Tansy here to direct her affection to, that was why, she decided pragmatically. Face it, you're at a vulnerable stage in your life. Ripe for a disastrous love-affair with the first attractive opportunist who comes along.

Vulnerable. Susceptible. Wise to remember that. Wise to remember, too, that a love-affair with this particular man could also have a devastating effect on the most precious and abiding thing left in her life, her relationship with Tansy.

Outside in the sunshine, exchanging smiles and hellos, both the vivid, disturbing memory of last night and the turgid musings in church seemed faintly ludicrous. The sea held its clichéd summer sparkle, the sky was an intense matching blue adrift with insouciant clouds.

The plump woman history student of last night had walked to church with a friend, and they gratefully accepted a lift back to the motor camp where they were staying in one of the cabins. On the way they talked excitedly about their courses and exchanged information about their blessedly absent families. Both had children variously engaged in work, study and extended overseas trips. One, his mother said sadly, was currently unemployed in spite of having a degree in social sciences.

The plump one politely tried to draw Fler into the conversation. 'You said you have a daughter at university? What is she doing?'

'BA majoring in history,' Fler told her. 'She's in the South Island at the moment on an archaeology dig with some other students.'

'That sounds interesting!' the other woman chimed in.

The plump one said, 'Is that the university group that Kyle—Mr Ranburn—was supposed to be leading?'

'What?' Fler's hands on the wheel were suddenly damp. She had a peculiar sensation in her chest. 'Where did you hear that?'

'Devina. You know Mr Hathaway was down on the programme for our course. The first day, someone asked why he hadn't been able to come, and she explained that he'd swapped at the last minute with Mr Ranburn. Personal reasons, she said. Perhaps Mr Hathaway has family down south, or something?'

Fler shook her head. 'I wouldn't know.' They'd swapped. Why? Kyle was supposed to have been leading the student party from Auckland? And Tansy must have known that. *Must* have!

Was that why she'd been so keen to go? Fler recalled her radiant face as she climbed on the bus.

Not over, after all.

She dropped off the two women at the motor camp, scarcely hearing their effusive thanks. Then she drove the car to the garage at the back of the guest house and entered through the kitchen.

Rae looked up from where she was seated at the big table, peeling apples. 'How was church?'

'Packed. The singing was nice.' She hadn't even heard the singing at the time, but now her memory recalled a fine, full chorus of 'How Great Thou Art'. Had she sung, too? She thought she must have.

'You look a bit bothered,' Rae told her. 'Want a cup of tea?'

'Yes. I'll make it. Apple pie at dinner?' She put down her bag to fill the kettle.

'Thought it would use up these apples,' Rae told her. 'OK?'

'Yes, of course.' Rae knew when to consult, when to use her initiative.

Her strong brown hands deftly carving a white path around another apple, Rae said, 'You look as though you could do with a day off. I'll hold the fort if you want to go away.'

Fler did that sometimes, but not usually during the summer school. It wasn't possible to have a real day or weekend off while staying around the guest house. If someone accosted her with a query or just wanting to talk, saying she was off-duty, however pleasantly, amounted to a rebuff.

'I'm all right,' she said. But maybe Rae had a point. A day away from Kyle Ranburn might be what was necessary to sort herself out. At the same time, she had an urgent desire to see him. To confront him with a question. *Why didn't you go to the South Island as planned?*

She made the tea, and Rae wiped her hands and picked up her cup. 'Kyle Ranburn was asking where you were. I think he wants to talk to you.'

Fler's hand, picking up her own cup, shook and spilled a dribble of hot tea on her fingers. She put down the cup and got up, turning her back to Rae while she tore off a paper towel from the rail on the wall to dab at her hand and then the table.

'Did he say what about?' she asked casually, resuming her seat.

'Nope. Wouldn't tell me. Said it was nothing to do with his room or anything.'

Unbidden, her skin recalled the firm, warm pressure of his fingers shackling her wrist. In her mind was the moon-painted sea and shared, breath-holding moments of sheer enchantment.

She sipped at the hot tea, welcomed its scalding heat on her tongue. Snap out of this dream. Get real.

Rae smiled at her, teasing. 'I think he fancies you.'

The odd lone commercial traveller or wayward husband trapped into a family holiday and hoping for a lucky distraction had elicited similar comments from Rae. Occasionally a less impossible contender would loom on the horizon and then Rae, happily married herself for thirty years to a big, shrewd, laughing and loving man, would have been happy to urge Fler in their direction if she'd shown the smallest interest.

Fler forced herself to smile back as lightly as always. In deference to Tansy's privacy, she had not told Rae the full story behind the suicide attempt, had named no names. 'I doubt it,' she said ruefully, hoping to sound convincing. 'More likely he's thought of something else he wants for his room or his classes, and doesn't think anyone will do but the top one on the totem. You're right, I'm not really in the mood to cope with any special requests today. Maybe I'll take you up on your offer.'

But she saw him when she was taking the car slowly down the drive to the gateway. Saw him in the side-mirror loping across the lawn with an air of purpose.

Several people were making their way on foot down the drive ahead of her, not hearing the car yet, and it would be patently rude deliberately to speed up and scatter them.

Then his hand was on the door frame where she had the window wound down, and she put her foot on the brake, glancing up at him with what she hoped was an air of cool enquiry.

'Going out again?' he asked.

'Yes. If you have any problems, I'm sure Rae will be able to deal with them.'

He gave a sudden amused grin. 'I doubt it.' He was looking at her searchingly. 'What's the matter?'

'Nothing.' She had her hand ostentatiously on the gear lever, letting her eyes flicker to the windscreen. A driver impatient at being delayed. 'I'll be away for the day.'

'Having a day off?'

'Yes.'

'You probably need it,' he acknowledged. 'Want company?'

She looked at him again, for a moment stupidly, impossibly tempted. She shook her head. 'No, thank you. Kind of you to offer.'

Ignoring the slight sarcasm, he said, 'Not kind.' His hand was still on the door. At last he removed it. 'Well, catch up with you later. Have a good day.'

Absurd to think the meaningless phrase sincerely meant, that on his lips it was a genuine wish for her.

She thanked him and sent the car down the slight slope again, acknowledging with a wave the parting of the group that was now near the wide gateway as they stood by to let her through.

She had made no plans. Probably she ought to have phoned, arranged to visit friends. But as she'd told Kyle, she didn't want company.

She drove aimlessly at first, discovered a back road that was unsealed and dusty but empty of traffic, parked the car and walked for several miles. Then she drove again and found herself in Whangarei, the streets baking hot and nearly deserted.

She bought a roll and some cheese and a smooth green-tinged banana and picnicked on the grass beside the Town Basin where the Hatea River widened to accommodate local fishing boats and pleasure yachts from home and overseas. There were craft there proudly declaring their origins in Sydney or Norfolk Island, France or Amsterdam. The *pohutukawa* that shaded her was already dropping scarlet spiky blossoms on the ground.

She visited one of her favourite places in Whangarei, a craft centre huddled into the embrace of a disused quarry, and bought a pottery bowl with a rounded, squat shape that pleased her, coloured and fired to a brilliant blue streaked pink and purple with an unexpected sandy, roughened accent near the shiny glazed rim. It reminded her of the sea below Manaaki on a blinding summer's day.

On her return she showed the bowl to Rae and said, 'I thought it would look good in the front lounge. Maybe on the table near the window.'

She carried it in there, and was halfway across to the window when she saw Kyle rising from one of the chairs.

'Don't get up,' she said, too late, halting with the blue bowl cradled in her hands before her.

'You're back.' He stood a few feet from her, giving her a look she couldn't read. He glanced at the bowl and said, 'That's a nice piece. Who made it?'

She gave him the name of the Northland potter who had crafted it, and continued past him to place it on a glass-topped table in the corner beside the long doors, removing a gleaming multi-coloured *paua* shell and a small carved wooden dolphin to make room. 'I just bought it,' she said to fill the silence. 'I thought this might be a good spot for it.'

'I'll enjoy looking at it while I'm talking tomorrow.' He ambled over to stand beside her, running a long, strong finger delicately over the glaze. 'Lovely,' he said. 'Where did you get it?'

She told him, and he said, 'I must visit there before I go home.'

'If you like pottery, you should. They have glass and other arts, too.'

'I notice you're a collector.'

She had about a dozen pieces placed about the public areas, and there were small pots or vases in all the rooms, inexpensive but chosen with care, the vases filled with fresh flowers every few days. 'I just buy those I can't bear not to have. When I can afford them.'

He smiled. 'I know that feeling. I've gone without a meal or two, in my younger days, to buy a piece of pottery—or a picture—that I felt was meant for me.'

'You collect pictures?'

'I don't have walls filled with them. Just a few that I like, that I wouldn't want to part with.'

Fler found herself wondering what sort of place he lived in. And whether he lived alone. He'd said he wasn't married. But he might live with other people. Flatmates, relatives . . . his mother?

Somehow she didn't think so.

Kyle said curiously, 'What are you thinking?'

'That you don't look like a mother's boy.'

He grinned, shook his head. 'What brought that on?'

She looked down at the shell and the carving in her hands. 'Just a random thought.' She ought not to have blurted it out. 'I'd better find homes for these.'

'I have a mother,' he said. 'I spent Christmas with her. She lives in Wellington.'

'Is that where you came from?' She didn't want to know this, she *didn't*. Small talk, that's all.

'Since I was ten. Before that we were in Auckland. I always had a sort of hankering to get back there.'

'What about your father?' It was a natural enquiry, expected. She was being polite, not asking out of any burning desire to know all about him—anything about him.

'He was a doctor. He died of a disease that he knew eighteen months before was going to kill him. That was a few years ago.'

'I'm sorry. Was it painful?'

'Sometimes. He could have got them to make it less so, but he wanted to have a clear mind for as long as possible. That was important to him. His choice.' He paused, and said, 'What about your parents?'

'My father died when I was twenty. Mum five years later.'

'Were you still married then?'

'Yes.' They'd never known about the divorce. If they'd been alive—but no. Not even to save her parents grief and worry and herself their inevitable disapproval, could she have gone on in that sham of a marriage.

And here she was exchanging personal information with a man who was—should have been—a perfect stranger.

She stepped back. 'I have things to do.'

She left him standing by the blue bowl, and when she looked back he was staring down at it, his finger idly tracing the smoothness of its rim, a small frown between his brows.

She'd missed the opportunity to ask him why he was here instead of at the dig in the South Island. They'd agreed not to talk about Tansy, she reminded herself. Not that it necessarily had anything to do with her.

Only she had a deep-down, sinking feeling that it was no coincidence.

Monday was a fine, still day with the odd cloud cooling the morning sun. Kyle's class voted to have their session down on the beach. The house seemed very quiet as Fler dusted and arranged fresh flowers and pencilled in a fresh booking at the desk. She realised that she missed the deep, incisive voice coming from the lounge.

He'd left several books on one of the tables in the big room for students to borrow or browse through. Moving them to wipe furniture polish over the table, she found her interest caught by one of the titles, and flicked over some of the pages.

She was absorbed in the print when Kyle's voice said, 'Borrow it if you like.'

She'd been so absorbed she hadn't heard him come in. She glanced at her watch, startled.

'It isn't lunchtime,' he assured her. 'They're taking a short break, but I came back to get one of those books I'd like to quote from.'

She closed the volume in her hand. 'This one...?'

'No.' He came over and picked up another from the table. 'You seem to be enjoying that.'

'Yes, I was.' Fler looked at the author's name on the dust jacket. 'She writes very vividly. The sandalwood traders had adventurous lives, didn't they?'

'They lived dangerously,' he agreed. 'Ever heard of Peter Dillon?'

'I heard you talking about him the other day. A bit of a buccaneer, wasn't he? It sounded fascinating.'

'Feel free to sit in on the class, if you like. I didn't know you were interested.'

'I didn't know it was your subject.' She saw the opportunity and took it, keeping her voice casual. 'What happened to Mr Hathaway?'

His gaze sharpened warily. 'He changed his mind. I am qualified to teach Pacific history. It makes a change.'

'You must have had to brush up on it. It was very short notice, wasn't it?'

There was a tiny pause. 'Yes, in the end. I've kept up with my reading, though. It's not too difficult.'

'Aren't you disappointed about not going to the dig down south?' she persisted. 'That is where you were supposed to be, isn't it?'

She was sure he'd tensed, although he didn't move. 'That didn't work out,' he said. His eyes met hers as though daring her to go on. When she didn't, he said, 'Who told you?'

'It's not a secret, is it? I thought it was common knowledge.'

'Of course it's no secret. Take the book. I think you'll enjoy it.' And he turned abruptly and went out.

She did enjoy it, and it whetted her appetite.

Returning it to him a couple of days later, she said, 'I sat up half the night reading it. I've made a list of some of the books in the bibliography so that I can request them from the library.'

'I could add a couple more for you,' he offered. 'If you're hooked on the subject.'

She was. The titles he suggested led them into more discussion of Captain Dillon and his contemporaries, and it wasn't until he offered to fetch from his room another book she might enjoy that she recalled she ought to be helping Rae in the linen room.

'I'll bring it down later,' he promised. 'I can leave it on the desk if you're not around.'

One afternoon when there was very little to do, instead of slipping away for a walk on the beach or some time in her own room, she unobtrusively seated herself in a chair by the door of the lounge and listened to Kyle talking about the interaction of European and Pacific cultures and how the desire for trade affected the attitudes of both towards each other.

He didn't look at her once while he spoke. When he said, 'That's all for today,' and the others began shuffling and stretching and moving towards the doors, she quietly left the room. But after dinner Kyle found her at the desk in the deserted hall.

'How did you like the lecture?' he asked. 'Were you able to follow it?'

'It was very interesting,' she said crisply, stacking a pile of papers neatly into a drawer. 'Why shouldn't I be able to follow it?' He didn't think she was stupid, did he?

'The course started almost two weeks ago,' he said. 'Coming in now, I thought you might have been a bit at sea.'

She hadn't realised how much she had learned from her absentminded listening-in. She'd understood most of his allusions to matters covered in previous sessions. 'No,' she said, 'you were very clear. I enjoyed it.' She locked the drawer and put the key into the pocket of her jeans.

A pleased light came into his eyes. 'Thank you.'

'I've always thought economics boring,' she confessed, 'but I never realised before how trade is interwoven with social history, or that the Pacific was such an important area for nineteenth-century commerce.'

'A lot of people don't. How are you getting on with the book I left for you?'

'I'm halfway through. Do you want it back?' She glanced around the desk and switched off the lamp that threw a pool of light on the work surface.

'No hurry. I'll let you know if I need it. Have you finished here for the night?'

'Yes,' she said thankfully. Everything was ready for morning. Rae had left for her home just down the road, and the kitchen staff were off until breakfast time. A murmur of voices came from the lounge where some of the guests were sharing a nightcap.

'I thought I'd go for a walk,' Kyle said. 'It's a lovely evening.'

'Yes.' The day had been hot, and the air inside felt stuffy and over-warm in spite of opened windows.

'Come with me,' he said. And then, as she made to give him an automatic refusal, he said in an oddly urgent undertone, 'Please!'

Her eyes flew to his face, and he smiled so that she thought she'd imagined the urgency. He shrugged. 'It's nicer with company. No one is likely to need you for the next half-hour or so. And you don't want to go to bed yet, do you?'

'I'll get a jacket,' she heard herself say. It was still balmy outside, but she knew that a cool night breeze might soon be lifting off the sea.

When she came back down the stairs he was by the door, waiting for her. She'd had to stop herself from pausing to put on make-up, merely grabbing the light cotton jacket out of her wardrobe and pushing her hair back with her fingers.

She thought she saw a hint of relief in Kyle's face when she joined him after switching on the telephone answering machine and leaving a small sign on the desk. She wondered if he'd thought she might change her mind.

Walking along the road side by side in the rapidly gathering dusk, they met Devina and one of the female students strolling back towards the bay, and exchanged greetings. It seemed to Fler that Devina gave them a rather sharp look.

'Am I going too fast?' Kyle asked a little later, glancing at her suddenly.

'No, I like a good pace,' Fler replied.

'My legs are longer than yours, though. Tell me if you want to slow down.'

They breasted a rise, and by mutual consent stopped to get their breath, turning to look towards the sea. Below them to the right was the guest house, its gables etched against the fading sky, and beyond that, lower down, the motor camp—a few tents, a row of cabins, several caravans. And of course, the sea, quietly rippling, a faint patina of pale gold on its surface from the dying sun.

To their left a shorn grass slope descended to a tangle of trees and shrubs and a couple of white posts indicated the beginning of a pathway.

'Where does that go?' Kyle asked.

'Another cove. It's pretty and very sheltered, but you can't swim there. At low tide you can walk around the rocks back to Manaaki that way.'

'It's low tide now, isn't it? Could we...?'

'Yes,' Fler answered. She hadn't done it for a long time. 'But it will be getting dark by the time we get back.'

'Can we make it in time?'

She glanced at her watch. 'I think so.' That way they were less likely to meet any more people than going back along the road. She refused to examine why that seemed a desirable thought.

The narrow path descended under a canopy of trees, coastal *karaka* and shaggy *kanuka*, not thick but casting a surprising amount of shadow, so that emerging from their gloom and finding it was still daylight after all was something of a surprise.

The sea had retreated past the black rocky buttresses enclosing the stony cove, exposing several outcrops rising from the pebble-littered sand.

'You'll have to take off your shoes if you don't want to get them wet,' Fler warned, shucking her rubber-soled canvas slip-ons.

Kyle untied his sneakers and knotted the laces to hang them about his neck.

The wet sand gave under their bare feet. When they reached the end of the rocks the water was still rippling in around their ankles. Rounding the point, they were in another small bay, this one filled with large grey stones and piled driftwood, and strands of pungent drying seaweed caught in whitened branches. There was a fan-shaped patch of soft pale sand about fifteen feet wide just above the stones. In the fold of a high smooth cliff yawned the black, narrow entrance to a cave, and Kyle said, 'That looks interesting.'

'It isn't very big,' Fler told him. 'But it's dark. You need a torch to explore it.'

She stood by while he peered into the blackness, then backed off from it to join her. He looked up at the cliff, the twisted, shaggy-barked *pohutukawa* trees and shiny falls of *taupata* clinging grimly to the sandstone. 'You can't get to this place at high tide, can you?'

'No. You wouldn't want to be stuck here.'

'The water wouldn't come as high as the cave, surely?'

'Only at certain times. Storms and the equinox.' She looked towards the water, the waves creeping almost silently up the sand. 'We'd better get moving.'

He laughed, walking at her side as she started towards the next headland. 'A fate worse than death?' he enquired. 'The prospect of being stuck with me between tides?'

'Hardly.'

After a moment he said thoughtfully, 'I don't know why I feel that wasn't meant to be a compliment.'

She said, 'The tide's turned. We'll have to go over the rocks here.' And paused to put on her shoes.

There was a rough kind of shelf worn by the water about six feet above the level of the sand. In places they had to scramble over uneven rocks and jump small crevasses. Kyle offered his hand but Fler shook her head. She had done this many times and she was naturally surefooted.

When they reached the beach below the guest house, the water was racing in past the rock on which they stood. They stopped to look down at it, and Fler said hopefully, 'The trick is to get in between waves. We'll have to wade, though.'

When she said, 'Now!' they both jumped down, the water up to Fler's knees. Then from nowhere a wave came hurtling in, almost throwing her off her feet as it thumped against her back, and sent her staggering into Kyle.

She gasped, and he clamped a firm arm about her waist and held her while they waded to the shore, the last few feet against the powerful undertow of the now receding wave.

It was, as Fler had predicted, nearly dark. At the water's edge she said breathlessly, 'Thank you,' and made to pull away from him. But he turned his head and looked down at her, his eyes gleaming, the deepening shadows turning his face hawklike. His hold tightened about her, and he bent his head, turned her fully into his arms, and kissed her.

# CHAPTER SEVEN

His lips were cool at first like the sea that washed around their feet. But they parted hers in a passionate invasion and then his warm breath was inside her mouth, and her whole body flamed into sudden desire.

The scent of his skin filled her nostrils, salt and musk, and her hand on his upper arm found the hard, firm muscle under taut skin. The arm about her waist drew her close so that her body curved to him, his heart beating against her breast, her thighs in their wet jeans cradled by his.

It was a long, timeless moment before Fler's mind exploded into action and she tried to thrust him away.

And another endless moment or two before he seemed to realise that she was fighting him, pushing against his chest, trying to twist her head aside.

When she wrenched her mouth from his he said, 'What?' in an almost dazed way, and slackened his arms.

Fler finally pulled out of his hold, and backed up the beach. Her voice shaking, she said, '*What on earth do you think you're doing?*'

He swallowed, shook his head, and came after her. He grinned suddenly. 'What do *you* think? Isn't it obvious?'

'Don't you touch me!' Fler said, her voice high and panicky.

Kyle stopped. 'You're surely not *frightened* of me?'

Of course she wasn't frightened. Except of her own reactions. She was disgusted.

Wasn't she?

70

'You're totally unscrupulous, aren't you?' she accused him.

It was so dark now that it was difficult to see his face, but he seemed to be thinking. 'I've never thought so,' he said. 'It was only a kiss. An impulse. I'm sorry if you're offended.'

A master of understatement. She was offended, shocked, nauseated. It didn't help that she could still taste his mouth on hers, still feel the imprint of his body.

As if he knew it, he said, 'I didn't get the impression that it was unwelcome...at first.'

'Of course it was unwelcome! What do you think I am?'

'I think you're a very attractive woman,' he said slowly. 'Are you afraid I'll imagine you're easy? I don't, you know.'

'Thank you. Is that a tribute to my integrity or to your sexual prowess?'

He laughed then, in a slightly exasperated way. 'I'm not claiming any particular prowess. Especially now. Don't you think the Sabine reaction is a bit extreme, in the circumstances?'

He had no morals at all. She couldn't cope with this. '*I think*,' she said, 'that you'd better keep your hands to yourself in future.' She turned towards the cliff path leading to the guest house, hampered by the rapidly falling darkness and the soft sand.

She knew he was right behind her all the way but neither of them spoke until they reached the top.

Then he said, 'If this has to do with Tansy——'

'We agreed not to mention her.'

'I know, but——'

'It was your idea,' she reminded him. And added, 'I should never have gone with you tonight. I ought to have known better.'

He gave a sharp sigh. 'Anyone would think I'm not safe to be let loose around women.'

'Are you?' Fler asked pointedly.

'You don't really believe I prey on every attractive woman who happens to be around?'

'Why shouldn't I believe it?'

Definitely annoyed now, he said, 'Because it isn't true!'

'Oh?'

The disbelief in her tone annoyed him further. She could see his anger in the very stillness of his body, the rigid angle of his jaw. 'You're determined to think the worst, aren't you?' he said finally. 'I've never been particularly fond of people with narrow, closed minds. I thought you'd be...at least mature enough to understand a few things, to listen to both sides of a story. But I was wrong, wasn't I?'

Then he swung away from her and strode towards the lighted doorway of the guest house.

The weekend came and went, and Fler hardly saw Kyle at all. Mostly he was in a group, and it was easy for him not to speak to her directly. On Sunday he told Rae he wouldn't be in for either lunch or dinner, and Devina left the same message. Fler spent the day with a peculiar, aching feeling in her throat. It was quiet as several of the tutors must have decided to get away for the day, and there were only three in for lunch.

She saw Kyle and Devina come in that evening, Devina for once looking slightly less then faultlessly groomed, her hair attractively tousled, a faint pink sunburn on her perfect nose, and her lipstick almost non-existent.

Kissed off? Fler found herself wondering, as Kyle entered behind her, carrying a large canvas bag. He too looked tousled, his hair uncombed, his shirt hanging loose and unbuttoned over creased shorts, and his feet bare.

Devina stopped a few feet inside the door and turned to him. 'If you give me my things I'll rinse them and hang them out before I go up.'

Kyle opened the bag and handed her a rolled towel that unravelled as he did so, spilling two pieces of minute bikini on to the floor. 'Sorry!'

Devina laughed, and they both bent, she picking up the pants, he the top. She took it from him and said, 'And my sweatshirt.'

He dug it out and she went off to the laundry near the kitchen. Kyle zipped the bag, swung it up in his hand and turned to see Fler behind the desk.

Their eyes met, and he hesitated.

'Have a good day?' she asked, the normal, polite enquiry of host to guest.

'Yes,' he said. 'Thanks.' His eyes were cool and challenging.

The door opened again and two more people entered, Conrad the art tutor and another man. They, too, looked a bit sunburned and both of them had towels slung over their shoulders and holdalls in their hands. With relief, Fler tore her eyes from Kyle's and smiled at them brightly. 'Had a nice day out?'

'Great,' they told her.

Conrad said, 'We went on a sailing trip. One of the locals offered.' He smiled at her, lingering as his companion went on up the stairs. From the corner of her eye, she saw Kyle follow. 'I suppose,' Conrad said, 'you've been working all day?'

Fler smiled back at him, determined not to let her eyes waver from his face. 'It's been quiet,' she said. 'Hardly anyone was here.'

Conrad ambled over to the desk and leaned on it. 'Had a bit of a holiday too, then?' He looked vaguely pleased.

'Certainly an easy day. You must find it tiring, tutoring six days a week.'

'Mmm. It's good though. They're an enthusiastic bunch.'

'Talented?'

'Some. What's important is that they enjoy it.'

Kyle must have reached the upper floor by now. She heard a door snap shut.

She locked a drawer and stood up. 'Most people seem to be enjoying their classes.'

Conrad strolled beside her as she made for the doorway marked 'Private' beyond the stairs. 'I suppose you haven't time to attend any yourself? Come and have a bash if you like.'

'Thank you. I sat in on one of Kyle's lectures, but I don't think I have any artistic talent.'

'You may not know until you try. Have a go.' He turned towards the stairs.

'Maybe I will.' She opened the door to her own quarters, smiling back at him. Conrad was a nice man, handsome and uncomplicated, and she wondered why his good looks failed to move her.

Maybe it was because he was married. A couple of letters had arrived for him, addressed in careful, childish printing on envelopes decorated with crayoned pictures and carrying cryptic messages. And another with his name on it in a clear feminine hand.

She was at the desk again the following evening when Conrad came down carrying a large envelope, and looked about as if checking that he was the only one in the lobby.

He said, 'I thought you might like this.' And handed her the envelope.

Mystified, she slid out the single sheet of stiff paper inside. And looked up at him in surprise.

'I hope you don't mind,' he said.

'When did you do it?' It was a pencil sketch in strong black lines of Fler, standing on the rocks below the guest house, against a background of climbing clouds, a breeze blowing her hair straight back and moulding her shirt to her torso, waves tossing about just inches from her feet. A few sweeping gulls completed the picture. She noticed the way her head was lifted, thought he'd exaggerated the chin slightly. Her figure leaned forward a little, legs parted and hands thrust into the pockets of her jeans.

She knew now exactly when he had done it. He'd captured her mood of determination not to allow herself to be carried away by emotion, to hold her independence, her self-respect.

Conrad shrugged. 'Saw you down there when I was mooching about the beach, trying to draw the waves. I thought you hadn't noticed me.'

'No, I didn't. It's very good. Are you sure you want me to keep it?'

'Seeing I didn't ask permission, I think you're entitled. And besides,' he grinned, not really meaning it, 'my wife might object to me keeping pictures of pretty ladies.'

He was an artist and she was almost sure his wife wouldn't have objected at all.

'Well, thank you, then,' she said. She didn't know what she was going to do with it. But it was nice that he'd wanted to give it to her. 'I'll find a place for it.'

She hoped he hadn't wanted it on public display. She'd have felt odd about that.

'Good,' he said. 'I'm glad you like it.'

*    *    *

She took it into her sitting-room and propped it against a photo of herself with Tansy as a twelve-year-old, while she decided what to do with it.

The last week of the summer school was in full swing now. The art and craft classes were preparing an exhibition of work to be held in the hall on the final Saturday, to which all the other students and their families were invited. Devina seemed to have time on her hands, and on Thursday when Kyle's students finished work for the day Fler glimpsed him and Devina going over the hill to the long sandy beach, towels swinging from their hands.

Gazing bleakly after them, she scarcely heard Rae asking, 'Are you coming down to the *marae* on Friday night?'

'What?' Fler turned.

'The Maori language group is going to welcome the rest of the summer school on to the *marae*, you know. And have a *hangi* meal and end-of-school party afterwards. You should come.'

'Should I?'

'Everyone else is, nearly.'

Fler smiled. 'Well . . . someone should stay here. You go. I already went to the barbecue.'

'That was ages ago. Do you good to get out. And all the guests will be down there. Tell you what, I'll get Hepi to come and watch this place for a while. He knows what to do if anyone comes or phones for a booking.'

That was true. Rae's teenage son had helped out sometimes at weekends when they were busy. 'Doesn't he want to go to the *marae*?'

'He says he's sick of all those speeches and everything. Boring, he reckons. The young ones, they've got no respect,' Rae said cheerfully.

\*   \*   \*

A formal *marae* welcome was a compliment to the recipients, and most of the students were conscious of the honour.

They gathered outside the gate of the *marae* in a large group, quietly talking, and waited until the *tangata whenua*, the home people, were ready to receive them.

Then everyone fell silent as a single woman's voice was lifted in a high, drawn-out call of, '*Haere mai, haere mai, haere mai*!' the last syllable falling at the end in a way that brought a tingle to Fler's nape.

The visitors began to move forward, and Fler saw that, surprisingly, the woman given the privilege of calling them on to the *marae* was white-skinned, one of the Pakeha students who had spent the last three weeks learning Maori language and customs.

Other voices soon joined her in singing a short welcoming *waiata*, and they were answered by a woman at the head of the visiting group, on their behalf. Only women were allowed to call visitors on to the *marae*, and only women were supposed to answer the call.

By the time the exchange was complete, the visitors were abreast of the rows of chairs set out facing the imposing carved entrance of the meeting house that faced. After a short pause they sat down while an elderly *kaumatua* with a carved stick in his hand gave the first welcoming speech. Then there were several speeches from male members of the *tangata whenua*—represented by both Maori and Pakeha students of all ages—and from the *manuhiri*, the visitors. Each speech was followed by a short *waiata*.

Kyle was one of those who spoke from the ranks of the *manuhiri*. Fler didn't understand all the Maori words but he appeared to be quite fluent.

When the formal welcome was over and the guests invited to mingle with the *tangata whenua*, shaking hands and pressing noses together in the traditional *hongi*, she found herself standing next to him, hemmed in by other people.

Face to face, they had to find something to say to each other.

'I didn't know you were a Maori speaker,' Fler said.

'Not a terribly good one,' he said. 'They asked me in desperation, I think.'

'False modesty?' she queried drily.

Kyle shook his head. 'Genuine shame. I've studied the language and the history, of course. In my field it's essential. But I wish I'd had more practice. I'd like to have done it better.'

'Kyle!' Devina appeared at his elbow. 'I need you. Can you come here a minute?'

Directing an apologetic smile at Fler, she took him off, and they disappeared into the throng as Rae appeared at her side. 'Everything all right?'

'Yes, of course.' Fler smiled determinedly. 'Why?'

'Oh, I don't know. You were looking a bit . . . wistful there, I thought.'

Fler shook her head. 'I was wishing I could speak Maori,' she said.

Rae laughed. 'All those speeches too much for you, eh?'

'Not at all,' Fler assured her. 'Only I'd like to appreciate them properly. I'm impressed that the students were able to take part in the welcome. It was great. But very unusual, isn't it?'

'There was a lot of discussion about letting them do it,' Rae told her. 'Some of us reckoned it would help them understand what they've been learning. But on the *marae* things have to be done right, and some people said it was disrespectful, just play-acting.'

'I think the students know how privileged they were,' Fler said. Several had been visibly nervous, and all had treated the occasion with due solemnity.

Rae nodded. 'A couple of the younger men were jealous. You know, they might be pretty old before they can stand on their home *marae* and speak for the people, especially if they have older brothers. But my auntie the *kuia* asked one of the students to *karanga* for her, and then the others gave in.'

'Are *you* jealous?' Fler asked curiously. Normally a woman had attained a certain age and status before having the right to call visitors on to the *marae*. And certainly she would be a member of the home tribe.

'I can wait,' Rae said. 'It's for my auntie to say. In a way it's safer for her to offer to stand down for a Pakeha woman for this one time than to do it for me.'

'In what way, safer?'

Rae explained. 'Sometimes when a *kuia* asks a younger woman to *karanga* for her, it goes to the young woman's head. She takes over and the *kuia* loses her *mana*, because she's given away her rights. I've seen a daughter do that to her mother. Young women can be very thoughtless sometimes. Too concerned with themselves. They have to learn to give back.'

'I don't think your aunt would be in any danger from you,' Fler said.

Food dug out of the ovens in the ground was served in the large dining hall. Conrad handed Fler a plate piled high with succulent wild pork, fresh seafood and sweet golden-fleshed *kumara*, and took a seat beside her. She saw Kyle sitting with his back to her at the next table, and concentrated her attention on the meal.

Afterwards she helped the dishwashers in the kitchen, then slipped away and walked along the road back home, the sound of guitars, singing and laughter gradually fading behind her.

Hepi looked up from the book he was reading, his feet propped on the desk. 'You're back early.'

'I'm a bit tired. Thanks for holding the fort, Hepi. No problems?'

'No probs,' he confirmed.

'They're still partying down there, if you want to go and join in,' she told him.

'Yeah? Any good?'

'Some pretty girls,' she told him, taking a note from the cash drawer and handing it to him.

'Y'reckon?' He grinned as he took the money with a word of thanks and got up, stuffing the paperback into a pocket and combing back his black hair with his fingers.

Fler smiled after him as he sauntered out. A nice lad, she thought. Rae wouldn't have too many worries with him.

For just a moment, she wondered with a little tug of sadness what it would have been like to have a son.

She left the door on the latch so that the latecomers could let themselves in, and, after pottering for a while at the desk and checking the kitchen and dining-room to make sure everything was ready for the morning, she locked the back door and made her way to her own room.

She had turned out the light and was drifting into sleep when she heard the faint crunch of footsteps on the shell-covered path outside her window.

Someone returning from the party? But they wouldn't come this way, past her private quarters.

Another footfall, and a thud against the window. She looked at it, saw only a dark square.

Then she heard the breathing. Harsh, heavy. Something thumped on the window again, scraped against the glass.

Fler got up and fumbled in the drawer at her bedside for a torch. She pulled on a cotton wrap-around dressing-gown over the big T-shirt she wore to bed, slipped her feet into canvas shoes and made for the front door.

Going around the building, she passed through an archway cut in vine-covered trellis to the small private lawn outside her window.

The garden by the house was slightly overgrown, and a young *pohutukawa* on the lawn overhung the pathway. She ran the beam of light over the garden, then up into the tree—and found a pair of eyes gleaming down at her.

'Hello,' she said. 'You're very cute, but I know your type. First it's heavy breathing, then Peeping Tomism, and next you'll be wanting to get into my room. And you'll turn nasty when I try to get rid of you. Or you'll be tap-dancing on the roof all night and keeping everyone awake.'

The furry possum clinging with hand-like paws on to a swaying branch didn't move. The big shiny eyes regarded her solemnly. A pointed pink nose twitched slightly.

'Off!' Fler said firmly, waving the torch. 'And don't come back!'

She'd probably dazzled the creature, she realised, and switched off the light, just as a male voice said, 'Very brave. But he doesn't seem impressed, does he?'

Fler gave a startled yelp and dropped the torch. The possum, a black furry shadow with a bushy uplifted tail, scurried into the higher branches of the tree, and Kyle said, 'Sorry, I didn't mean to scare you.'

'Well, you did!' Fler told him crossly, futilely gazing round in the dark for the torch. 'What on earth are you doing, creeping about like that?'

'I wasn't. I was just coming in when I saw you going round the side in your——' he paused '—*déshabillé,*' he drawled at last. 'I could think of only two reasons for that, and it seemed unlikely that you were going to meet your lover. I figured if you were after an intruder you might need some help. Though it sounded as if you had your own way of dealing with it,' he added drily. 'Possibly not very effective if it had been a real Peeping Tom—or worse.'

'It's only a possum.'

'Did you know that when you came out?'

'I was fairly sure.'

'What if you were wrong?'

'Then I'd have scared him off.' Thinking she saw the gleam of the torch on the ground, she took a step towards it, and felt something roll under her foot—she'd been mistaken, she realised, that was the torch she'd just stepped on—and crashed heavily to the ground on her hip and elbow.

Kyle dived forward too late to save her. He went down on one knee as she gasped with pain. 'Are you hurt?'

'Yes.' She sat up, nursing the elbow. '*Hell*!' She seldom swore, but the pain was fierce. She felt dizzy, and the blackness of the night seemed to have intensified.

He fumbled at her arm. 'Where's the damn torch?'

'I stepped on it,' Fler said, gritting her teeth. 'Your fault,' she added with irrational irritation.

He gripped her uninjured arm with one hand and put his other arm about her waist. 'Can you stand?'

'Yes. I think so.' Her hip throbbed, but she didn't think she'd broken anything.

He helped her up, and she took a couple of deep breaths of the night air. He still had an arm about her waist. She didn't suggest he remove it. Right now she needed all the support that was available.

She tried to walk, limping a bit, doing her best to ignore the way the world seemed to be rolling slowly round. After a few steps Kyle said, 'Here,' and swung her up into his arms.

Fler made no objection. She was too busy trying to hold on to the remnants of consciousness.

Even with her eyes closed she was aware of him going up the front steps and thrusting the door wide with his shoulder, then striding through the lighted lobby to the door marked 'Private'. He stopped there and said, 'Fler? Can you open it?'

She fumbled with the handle and he pushed his way inside and found the sofa in the light spilling through the open door. Thankfully, she felt the sofa under her, the cushions behind her head, heard the door close and she thought he'd gone.

But then the room was flooded with light, making her blink, and Kyle was back at her side, saying, 'Where's your bathroom?'

'Across the passage,' she muttered.

The dizziness was receding, thank heaven, but she was grateful for the cool damp cloth that he placed on her forehead when he came back.

'You hurt your arm?' he said. 'Let's have a look.'

She let him push up the sleeve of her robe, and moved the limb when he asked her to try, wincing at the pain. 'It's not a sharp pain,' she said. 'It isn't broken. I'll live.'

'I think you're right,' he said. 'But you're already developing a hefty bruise. It'll be stiff for a day or two. You were limping as well.'

'Just another bruise, I'm sure. Thanks for helping. I'll be fine, now.'

'I'm not leaving you yet. You still look rather sheet-like.'

'Gee, thanks!' Fler murmured, putting up a hand to adjust the cloth as it slipped on her forehead. 'Your bedside manner is very polished.'

Kyle grinned. 'If it's any comfort, you're also looking fairly seductive. I'll freshen that for you,' he offered, taking the cloth from her and heading back to the bathroom.

Fler realised then that the gown had parted over her legs, leaving most of their length exposed to view. She half sat up to cover them before he came back. Kyle glanced down at the modest readjustment as he handed her back the cloth, and although his mouth twitched up at the corners he said only, 'I'm sure you could do with a drink—something hot, or do you keep liquor for medicinal purposes?'

'You needn't——'

'I want to. You did say it was my fault.'

'That wasn't fair,' she admitted. 'You were only trying to help.'

'Hmm,' he said, his eyes skimming her. 'Some help.'

Fler gave a small laugh, and he grinned down at her. 'What'll it be? Coffee, tea—what?'

'Coffee,' she said. Probably the wrong thing, but it was what she felt in need of. 'Thanks. There's instant in the cupboard to the left of the stove.'

'I'll find it. Milk and sugar?'

'No milk, one sugar. Have some yourself.'

When she'd had the coffee she felt much better. Putting the cup on the floor beside her, she saw that Kyle, his empty mug cradled in his hands, was staring at the drawing still propped against the photograph where she had left it.

'Thank you,' she said.

He brought his gaze back to her. After a moment he rose and picked up her cup. His eyes drifted back to the sketch. 'Conrad?' he asked.

'Yes.' She felt herself flushing. She was embarrassed, he'd been looking at it so intently. There was something revealing about the drawing, she knew. Something Conrad had caught that she wouldn't want the whole world seeing.

'It's good,' he said. His eyes returned to hers, searchingly. 'You know he's married?'

Fler blinked. 'Of course I know.' Indignant at the absurd implication, she said, 'Does that have anything to do with you?'

His face closed. 'No,' he agreed. 'I guess not.' He turned abruptly and took the cups to the kitchen. She heard him clatter them into the sink and run the water.

By the time he returned she was sitting up properly, her feet on the floor. So far the room had stayed reassuringly still.

'Do you need help to get into bed?' he asked.

'No. I'll be OK now.'

'I'll find the torch for you in the morning,' he offered.

'Thank you. And thanks for the help.'

'The least I could do,' he told her. 'Sure you'll be all right?'

'Quite sure.' Her ears alerted to sounds from outside. 'Someone's coming in, I think. The party must be breaking up.'

'Then I'd better go,' he said, 'before I compromise you.' His eyes gleamed with humour.

At the door he paused. 'You wouldn't like me to send Devina or one of the other women in to you?'

'No! Thanks, but really, I don't need anyone. It's only a couple of bruises.'

'OK,' he said, turning the handle. 'See you in the morning.'

# CHAPTER EIGHT

WATCHING the door close behind him, Fler experienced an odd feeling of let-down. A couple of minutes later there were voices in the lobby, the hallway. She carefully got off the sofa, went to her bathroom and then slid into bed, adjusting herself so that the bruised hip and arm were reasonably comfortable.

The possum was still in the tree, she remembered. If it stayed around she'd have to see about getting it trapped and disposed of. The animals were not native to New Zealand, and they were devastating the *pohutukawa* trees along the coast, besides being terribly destructive of gardens and fruit trees, and carrying diseases that could be passed to cattle, infecting milk supplies.

She woke painfully several times after changing position in her sleep, and when she got up had trouble dressing. She had struggled into her jeans and a sweatshirt and was trying to comb her hair left-handed when she heard a crunch on the path outside and a shadow fell across the window.

She pulled back the net curtains and raised the sash. Kyle stood there with the torch in his hand.

'Does it work?' she asked him.

'Yes. None the worse for wear.' He came over to the window and handed it to her. 'How are you feeling?'

'Stiff, as predicted. Otherwise, fine.'

She glanced up at the *pohutukawa*, and he followed her gaze. 'No sign of your nocturnal visitor,' he said. 'I think he's scarpered.'

'I hope so.' A little worriedly, she scanned the branches again. 'I don't want to have to have him killed.'

'Softie,' he mocked.

'Yes, I am,' Fler admitted cheerfully. 'I actually quite like the little beggars. But I know they're pests.'

'Sometimes,' he suggested, 'I think you feel much the same about me.'

She stared at him wordlessly.

Kyle laughed. 'Don't look so shocked. It isn't a sin to like someone. Even if you do think they ought to be boiled in oil for the good of their souls.'

Finding her voice, Fler said, 'I wouldn't boil anyone in oil.' It sounded perfectly horrible, if one thought about it. Not a fate she'd wish on her worst enemy. Which Kyle wasn't—was he?

He said, 'No, but *you're* a softie. We already know that, don't we?'

His head was cocked to one side, a smile lurking at the corners of his mouth. In the morning light and with that expression on his face he looked devastatingly attractive.

Fler forced her heart to harden. 'Not that much of a softie,' she said primly, and closed the window on the sound of his laughter.

The history class had a wrap-up session that morning, leaving the students free to leave or to visit the art exhibition in the afternoon.

As they were preparing the tables for lunch, Rae told Fler, 'Kyle Ranburn's booked in for an extra week.'

'He's *what*?'

Rae looked at her in surprise. It wasn't so unusual for one or two tutors or students to decide they didn't want to leave yet. If they had some more holiday to spend, what better place than a quiet beachside guest house? 'It's all right, isn't it? We've got a family coming in on Monday, I know, but his room wasn't booked.'

'I just . . . thought he'd have to get back to Auckland.'

'Term isn't starting until March.'

'Yes, but they have meetings and things beforehand,' Fler said lamely. 'Don't they?'

'Do they? I wouldn't know. Anyway, he wants to stay on. He said something about maybe helping out because he's got a guilty conscience. What was he on about?'

Fler didn't know why she had omitted mentioning Kyle when she explained to Rae the reason for her limp and the uselessness of her right arm this morning. Reluctantly, she said, 'He gave me a fright last night when I was outside trying to shoo off the possum. That's when I dropped the torch. But it wasn't his fault. He thought I might need rescuing from a prowler.'

'Oh, I see.' Rae shot her a curious look. 'He seems nice.'

'Don't get any ideas,' Fler said, more sharply than she'd intended. 'He's not my type.'

'What is your type?'

'I doubt if there is one.' Fler made to lift a water jug from the sideboard and nearly dropped it. 'Ouch!' She'd forgotten about her arm.

'I'll take that.' Rae picked it up. 'Maybe you can do with an extra hand or two.'

Kyle lingered as the others left the table after lunch. 'Are you planning on going to the exhibition?' he asked Fler.

'Probably.' But walking to the hall was not an inviting prospect with her bruised and painful hip, and she didn't fancy driving with her elbow as it was.

'I'll take you,' he offered. 'We can use my car.'

'Well, that's kind of you, but——'

'Atonement,' he said. 'I believe there's some interesting pottery down there.'

'You've nothing to atone for. And I can't afford to buy any more pots just now.'

'But you like looking, don't you? Come on, allow me to salve my conscience.'

Rae, busy lifting a cloth from one of the tables, said, 'Go on, Fler. You're not a lot of use with that arm, anyway. I can manage here.'

Fler shot her a look which she totally ignored. 'All right,' she capitulated. 'Thank you.'

Kyle gave her a glinting grin and said soothingly, 'There, that didn't hurt, did it?'

Most of the pottery was passable, and a few pieces looked quite professional. Others, though a bit rough, were ambitious and interesting. While a good many were for showing only, about half bore price tags.

Fler lingered over a large shallow dish, the colour of sand under water, the impression heightened by a shiny glaze. Understated among more flamboyant colours, textures, and shapes, it stood out for the simplicity of its form and execution. She peered at the price, and regretfully moved on through the crowd.

At her side, Kyle said, 'It's a nice piece.'

'Mmm. Too dear for me, though.' She had a collection of small shells which she kept in a large glass jar. It occurred to her that they'd look much better in the sand-coloured dish, more at home. She cast a longing glance over her shoulder, but it was only a couple of weeks since she'd bought the blue bowl. No more extravagances for a while. She worked to a tight budget, and Tansy's education was becoming more and more expensive.

They stopped before a large painting of the bay, with the hills and the guest house lovingly delineated.

'You should buy that, Fler.' A local man stopped beside them, regarding the picture appreciatively.

'Won't fit in my budget, Jack,' she told him. Then, teasing, 'Did you paint it?'

He shook his head. 'Nope. But the missus was in Conrad Duncan's class. She's got a picture here somewhere of the cowshed. Beats me why she didn't do one of the house.'

He wandered off, and Fler returned her attention to the picture before her. 'Is it any good?' she asked Kyle.

'Why don't you ask Conrad?'

'Don't you know?'

He looked down at her. 'I'm not an art expert. But I have an opinion, if that's what you want.'

'That's what I want.'

'Well...it's competent. A good amateur painting. Unambitious. Do you like it?'

'Not a lot.' She looked back at it again. 'I think I'll pass on Jack's suggestion.'

'Now there,' he said, stopping at another, smaller painting, 'is something.'

'You like abstract art?' She stared at the square of apparently jumbled colours. It didn't look like anything, but she sensed a feeling of contained power, of brushstrokes that had a sense of disciplined purpose behind them.

'I think it's pretty good.'

'I believe you,' Fler told him.

He laughed. 'You don't think so?'

She didn't suppose her opinion counted for anything, but she said, 'Yes. But unlike you, I have no idea why.'

He gave her a succinct résumé of his reasons, and then said, 'But Conrad could tell you a lot more.'

'Conrad's busy at the moment,' Fler pointed out. As art tutor, he was naturally heavily involved in the organisation of the exhibition, and since they'd arrived he'd been constantly moving through the crowd, talking almost nonstop. 'Besides, he's so wrapped up in his subject he does tend to go on a bit.'

Kyle cast her a curious glance. 'Most women don't seem to mind that.'

Fler raised her brows.

'Even I can see that he looks like God's gift,' Kyle said.

'As you told me last night, he's married,' Fler pointed out. 'Besides, looks aren't everything. Actually he doesn't make my heart go pitterpat the least bit.'

'Do *I*?' Kyle asked curiously.

He sounded as though he really wanted to know. Floundering, she looked about them to ensure they weren't being overheard. 'Vanity,' she said tartly, 'will get you nowhere.'

She walked on, but he said in her ear, 'Tell me what will, then?'

Fler shook her head, and was relieved to be rescued by another local resident who stopped to chat.

When they had seen everything and talked to several people, Kyle led her back to the car and opened the door. As she settled into her seat he said, 'Excuse me for a couple of minutes. I'll be right back.'

When he returned he was carrying something wrapped loosely in brown paper. Not a picture, it was too bulky for that. Puzzled, Fler bit back the enquiry on the tip of her tongue. It was none of her business what he'd bought.

He said carelessly as he slid in behind the wheel, 'Hold that for me, would you?'

She sat with it in her lap until he'd turned the car and driven up the long slope to the top of the cliff, where a fence had been erected and there was a place for people to park and admire the view. Swinging the car in and coming to a stop within feet of the fence, he said, 'Open it.'

Suspicion became more than that. 'It's yours,' she said firmly.

'No. It's yours. In reparation, if you like. And to say thanks for a great three weeks. Open it.'

'You can't buy me presents...'

'I did. Go ahead.'

Of course she knew what it was. Slowly she folded back the paper and revealed the glazed, sand-coloured dish. 'You can't do this, Kyle,' she said again. 'I can't accept it from you.'

'I won't take it back,' he said, and turned the key in the ignition.

'Kyle——'

'I'm sorry.' He switched the key off again. 'I don't want to force anything on you. I hoped——' he made a strange little gesture with his hands, turning them palm-upward '—it would please you. No strings, I swear. But if it makes you uncomfortable, forget it. I'll find a home for it, or you can, if you like.'

She looked into his face and saw that this was no bid to make her feel guilty. He really meant it. She said, 'I love it, you know I do. It was generous of you. I—well, thank you.'

'OK,' he said. And unexpectedly leaned over to quickly, lightly kiss her mouth. 'No strings,' he said again, and started the car, driving slowly the rest of the way home.

She wondered if he meant the dish, the kiss or both.

Not that it had been a real kiss, she reassured herself. It had lasted less than half a second. But it had left a warm tingling feeling on her lips that seemed to spread softly, gently all over her body.

\* \* \*

The place became strangely quiet with the ending of the summer school. Kyle had meant what he'd said about helping out. He appeared at Fler's elbow when she was changing linen in the bedrooms and asked what he could do.

'There's no need,' she said. 'I'm just stripping these. Rae or one of the girls will come and make them up later.'

But he gathered up the linen and carried it to the laundry for her. And later he insisted on being the one to peg the washing on the big rotary line behind the house.

'You don't use a dryer?' he asked, as Fler stood by, redundant. He was making a surprisingly good job, obviously no novice at the task.

'We try not to,' she said. 'It wastes electricity, and the sheets seem fresher if they're dried in the sun. You know, you are not responsible for my accident.'

'At the time you said I was.'

'You know I didn't mean it. I can't charge you board and have you working for me.'

'Don't worry about it. I'm enjoying myself.'

Fler shook her head, but he wasn't to be deflected from his self-inflicted penance. She got used to having him appear at her side, quietly taking loads, completing small tasks that she awkwardly attempted, generally making life easier.

The family who arrived on Monday and the other guests who followed spent nearly all their time either at the beach, on the water or touring around in their cars, and except at breakfast and dinner Manaaki was almost deserted. Sometimes when Rae and the others weren't needed Fler and Kyle were the only two in the place.

Finding her one afternoon struggling to trim back a vine from one of the windows, he took the secateurs that she was clumsily wielding with her left hand. 'Why didn't you ask me to do that?' he demanded, making short work of the intrusive tendrils.

'I could have done it.'

He glanced at her. 'Were you always this independent?'

'If I wasn't before, I've certainly learned to be in the last five years.'

'Since your divorce?' He snipped at a wiry green strand he'd pulled away from the window frame.

'Yes.'

'Was that when you bought this place?'

'Sort of. Rick and I were supposed to be running it together. Then our marriage . . . fell apart just as we were about to move in. Eventually we decided that I'd keep it.' Rick had never been an ungenerous man.

'And you made a go of it on your own?'

'With some help from the bank. And I was lucky to find Rae. She's been wonderful.'

'It can't have been easy for you.'

Fler shrugged. 'What's ever easy?'

'Have you never thought of marrying again?'

She gave a small laugh. 'Why should I?'

'Why not?'

'I'm doing all right on my own,' she said firmly, stooping to gather up the pieces of the plant that he'd trimmed. 'I'll put these on the compost heap.' And as he moved to help, 'No, it's all right, I can manage, thanks. They're not heavy.'

By the end of the week the staff had begun to treat Kyle as one of themselves. Fler had slipped into a half-exasperated, half-amused kind of companionship with him. Although the school was finished, by tacit consent they had extended their pact not to mention Tansy. One day he told her about his family, the brother and sister who with their young children shared the family Christmases in Wellington.

'You're lucky,' she said. 'I always wanted brothers and sisters. I'd have liked to provide some for Tansy, too.'

His suddenly rigid expression halted her there. She bit her lip, and after a small silence Kyle began lightly talking about something else.

On Friday night they sat on the front steps together watching the sun go down. Kyle asked, 'Will you miss me when I go?'

'Are you fishing?' she asked, surprised at the sharpness of her dismay, but hiding it behind a smile.

He smiled back. 'Will you?' he persisted.

'You've been very useful,' she said. 'Thank you, but I'll be fine now.' She flexed her elbow. It hardly hurt at all. 'I'm quite back to normal.'

His smile turned a little ironic. 'You don't like to give anything away, do you?'

Warily, she said, 'I don't know what you mean.'

He regarded her a moment longer, sighed and looked away from her, staring at the orange glow on the water reflecting the sky. He studied his hands, loosely linked between his knees, and then lifted his head as though about to say something more.

Briefly visited by a premonition, Fler said, 'When are you leaving?'

He turned his head. 'Must you sound so eager?'

'I wasn't... aware of sounding eager.'

'Sunday,' he told her. 'I have to be back in Auckland for a meeting on Monday morning.'

He sounded slightly fed up, and she thought that she'd been ungracious. 'We'll all miss you,' she said. 'You've been very helpful. It wasn't necessary, but I'm grateful.'

She got up to go inside, but he lifted a hand and caught her wrist, looking up at her. 'I wanted to know,' he said, 'whether you *personally* will miss me.'

All this week he'd been a helping hand, a friend in need. Nothing else. She'd pushed their previous differences and the reasons for them to the back of her mind, content to accept the practical aid he offered, and share a temporary friendship. Ignored the occasional tingling pleasure she experienced when their hands brushed, or when she caught the male fragrance of his skin, or saw him impatiently push back his hair as he bent to some task.

'It can't possibly matter,' she said.

Still holding her wrist, Kyle stood up, facing her. His hazel eyes searched hers. 'It matters to me,' he said gently. 'Are you sure it doesn't to you?'

Fler shook her head, her mouth dry. 'I'm sorry,' she said, and tugged her wrist from his grasp.

'Fler!' As she made to go inside, he caught her shoulder and spun her into his arms, locking them about her while he stared down into her face. His own looked taut and obdurate. 'I want to see you again,' he said.

She quelled the eager leap of her heart. Keeping her voice steady, she answered, 'I don't think that would be a good idea.'

An almost calculating look entered his eyes. 'Maybe I can persuade you it would.'

His mouth was on hers before she could take any evasive action, and when she pushed against him she discovered how strong his arms were, holding her still without any great effort.

Her lips were responding to the insistent warmth of his kiss, and her body reacting to the closeness of his. She could feel his breath on her cheek, and when she opened her eyes, she saw his were closed, dark lashes lying on his tanned cheek, his hair falling over a forehead faintly sheened with fine sweat.

When his mouth left hers it wandered to her cheek, then down to the curve of her neck and shoulder. And she finally managed to say chokingly, 'Kyle, *don't*!'

His breathing was harsh, and he refused to let her go, but he raised his head and looked at her. 'Is it Tansy?' he asked tensely. 'Maybe it's time we talked about that.'

Then the telephone inside rang, and Fler said, 'I'll have to answer that.'

'Rae——'

'She's gone home for the night. There's no one else. Let me go, Kyle.'

Reluctantly he loosened his grip, and she hurried inside.

He followed her, watching while she dealt with the call and took a reservation in for the following month.

The phone rang again almost as she put down the receiver, and she cast him a look of apology and turned to lift it again.

'Mum?'

Fler swallowed. Her eyes flew to Kyle, a sudden irrational guilt flooding through her. She felt naked, caught, as though Tansy could see the man standing beside her, his eyes intent on the consternation in her face.

'Just . . . just a minute, darling,' she said, her voice husky with the effort of keeping it steady. 'I'll switch the phone through to my room.'

Kyle lifted his brows as she pressed the button. 'It's . . . private,' she said. 'My daughter.' She looked almost defiantly at him.

His expression was wooden as he stepped back. 'Don't tell her I'm here,' he said in a low, urgent tone.

Fler stopped short. She realised that for a moment all
she'd thought of was concealment, keeping the knowledge of his presence secret from Tansy.

She went past him without a word.

Her hand was damp as she picked up the phone by
her bed. 'Is everything all right, Tansy?'

'Yes, I s'pose. I'm not sick or anything. Just wanted
to talk to you.'

She sounded forlorn, and with the recent memory of
her lying unconscious in hospital, Fler felt a clutch of
fear. 'Are you sure there's nothing wrong?'

'No, nothing, honest. Just...the dig isn't quite...you
know, as interesting as I thought it would be.'

'That...that's too bad,' Fler commiserated. Because
Kyle isn't there? she wondered.

'Did you get my postcards?'

'Yes, thank you.' There'd been two, with brief, un-
informative messages. 'Did you get my letters?'

'Yeah. Summer school go all right?'

'Fine,' Fler said brightly. 'Everyone had a great time.
They're all gone now, though.' All but Kyle. Did she
*know*? Did Tansy know he was here, that there'd been
a swap?

'Good. I miss you.'

Fler swallowed a lump in her throat. 'I miss you, too.'

'I meant to write last week, but you know, time goes
by...so I thought I'd phone and let you know I'm OK.'

'I'm glad you did. You didn't even make it a collect
call!' she teased.

Tansy laughed. 'How's everyone there? Anything
happening?'

'No. Nothing much. One of Rae's nieces is getting
married next weekend. Do you remember Hine?'

'Um, yeah, I think so, from high school. Is the guest
house very busy? Are you booked out?'

'No, not really busy. We've only one family staying, and another coming tomorrow.'

'Uh-huh. No one interesting?'

*Did* she know? Was she trying to find out something?

As Fler hesitated, Tansy said, 'My phone card's about to run out. You're expecting me a few days before term starts, aren't you?'

'Yes, it's nice to hear your voice, and it'll be lovely to have you home, even for a little while.' Shocked, Fler realised that part of the warmth in her voice was feigned.

'I might——'

But the rest of the sentence was swallowed in pips and then silence.

Fler slowly put down the receiver. Tansy sounded all right, she assured herself. Didn't she? What had those questions meant?

Nothing. Just the kind of questions anyone asked when they had nothing to say but wanted to hear a loved, familiar voice.

She shook herself and got off the bed to return to the lobby. Kyle was still standing where she'd left him.

He looked at her questioningly. 'Problems?'

'No.' Fler shook her head. You are the problem, she thought.

Something in his face relaxed. 'She's OK, then?'

'She said she's fine.'

'We need to talk, Fler——'

'Mrs Daniels!'

The mother of the family that was staying the week came running down the stairs. 'Mrs Daniels, I'm sorry— my son's been sick all over the bedroom. I'll need clean sheets, and a bucket and cloth.'

In the end they needed more than that. After she'd helped clean up the mess Fler called a doctor and, when he'd examined the boy, spent some time answering questions about the day's menu. It appeared the child might have some form of food poisoning, and his sister looked like developing the same symptoms.

Then she returned to doing what she could to help the distraught parents. By the time she was able to think about anything else, Kyle took one look at her and said, 'You'd better get some sleep. You look like death.'

Fler went to bed after switching the phone through to her room in case the family needed her. But it was a long time before she slept. The thought of food poisoning was a real worry. Any hint that it was connected with the guest house could ruin her business.

By a process of elimination, it was decided that the contamination had probably been in some fast food the family had picked up on a day trip to Whangarei. Fler breathed a sigh of relief, but she had little time to savour it, for an influx of weekenders arrived before lunch on Saturday, and because Rae and some of the part-time staff were involved in the wedding at the *marae* she was rushed off her feet.

The children had stopped being sick but she was carrying a tray of specially prepared light food upstairs when Kyle waylaid her.

'Can I take that?' he offered.

'No, I want to talk to the mother, anyway.'

'When will you have time to talk to me?' he asked her.

Harrassed and tired, she said, 'Leave me *alone*, Kyle!'

He drew back as if she'd hit him. 'Of course,' he said coolly. 'If that's what you want.'

She hesitated, caught by something in his face, but he turned from her and continued on down the stairs, and after a moment she carried on up them.

# CHAPTER NINE

SHE made sure there was no opportunity to talk further before Kyle left on Sunday. He knew, of course. His face took on a look of bleak, frustrated anger, but he didn't force the issue.

When hollow panic seized her at the thought of his departure, she'd tell herself to stop behaving like an adolescent with a silly crush on a man. She scarcely knew him. Keep it that way. A couple of kisses and some entertaining conversations didn't mean anything. There was nothing between them that amounted to any kind of affair. And when he got back to Auckland he'd no doubt find plenty of younger, more receptive women eager and waiting.

'Give my regards to Devina,' she said, scribbling a receipt as he stood at the counter, his bags on the floor at his side.

'Why Devina, particularly?' he asked.

Because Devina's face had come to mind when she thought about the women he was going back to. 'Won't you be seeing her?' Fler asked, twisting the knife in her own surprising pain.

'I might.' He regarded her narrowly. 'I didn't think you two were particularly friendly.'

Fler shrugged. Had he noticed that she'd felt a humiliating jealousy of the younger woman? Please, no! 'I thought she was nice.' That was true. Devina had always been perfectly friendly and pleasant. Fler had been hypersensitively convinced that her sunny apologies as she hooked an arm into Kyle's and led him off somewhere indicated that she regarded Fler as no possible rival.

She handed him the receipt and gave him an impersonal smile. 'Thank you. Come and stay with us again.'

'Do you mean that?'

It was her usual farewell speech to the guests, and he must know that. Her smile wavered. 'Of course.'

'I might take you up on it,' he said, tucking the receipt into his pocket. As she told herself unconvincingly that it wasn't a threat, he picked up one of the cards from the desk and put that in his pocket, too. Then he stood looking at her as though debating something in his mind. But someone came noisily in through the front door, and he picked up his bags, nodded rather ironically to Fler and went out.

The newcomer approaching the desk took all her attention, and she didn't even hear Kyle's car drive out of the car park.

Fortunately the next few weeks were unusually busy. And yet Fler was amazed at how much she missed Kyle's presence, his quiet humour, his way of being on hand when help was needed, the faint gleam of interest in his eyes when he looked at her.

Be honest, she said to herself one night as she lay wakeful and restless, on a night too warm for sleep. You find him dead sexy. You wanted him.

She turned on her side, threw off the blanket and punched a hand into her pillow. You and how many others?

Tansy, for one. A familiar sick feeling churned in her stomach. He'd wanted them both, briefly. First Tansy, then her.

*She's too young for him, anyway.* The thought had surfaced, unbidden.

She threw herself on to her back, appalled, staring at the darkened ceiling. Was she jealous of her own daughter?

*Yes*, came the spontaneous answer.

She closed her eyes. 'He's not worth it,' she muttered aloud. For a while she'd fallen under the potent spell of that understated sexuality. But no man was going to come between her and Tansy. Certainly not one with as few scruples as Kyle Ranburn.

The day before Tansy was due back, she said to Rae, 'Would you do something for me? Please don't mention Kyle to Tansy.'

Rae was surprised. 'She's a big girl. You're entitled to have a man in your life, Fler.'

'Not that man!' Fler hesitated, then said, 'Rae, Kyle was the reason she took those pills last year.'

'*Kyle* was?'

'Don't let her know I told you.' She'd never broken a promise to Tansy before, never deceived her. She felt a surge of anger against Kyle. But for Tansy's sake it was best she didn't know he'd been here.

'Do you want me to swear the staff to secrecy?' Rae asked.

'No.' Fler's teeth worried at her lower lip. 'We can't do that. I'll just have to hope they don't happen to mention his name.'

When she alighted from the bus, Tansy looked tanned and healthy, but the eager glow that she'd gone off with had disappeared. She hugged Fler extravagantly and seemed glad to be home.

Sitting on her mother's bed that night with a cup of a hot cocoa in her hand, she talked at random about the dig, her plans for the year, her childhood.

Fler watched her affectionately, catching a breath at the loveliness of her, the sheen of freshly brushed pale hair, the sweet, smooth curve of a cheek, the childish unselfconsciousness of Tansy's pose, long brown legs curled under her, both hands wrapped about the fat white mug that held the cocoa. She might have been twelve years old again.

At last she uncurled herself and kissed Fler goodnight, asking teasingly, 'Want me to tuck you up?'

Fler laughed and kissed her back. 'Goodnight, darling.'

Tansy stepped back. 'Do you ever miss Daddy?'

'Sometimes,' Fler answered truthfully. She wondered if Tansy still blamed her for the divorce. For a while it had been a real problem, Tansy's savage resentment. Fortunately, Rick had supported Fler, not giving Tansy any fuel for it. Of course, he'd been fairly desperate not to have to assume custody of her, himself. 'I'm sorry, Tansy,' she said for the hundredth time, 'that we couldn't work it out. You miss him a lot, don't you?'

Tansy shrugged. 'I've got over it now. See you in the morning.'

It would have been a real joy having her home for those few days, if Fler hadn't been constantly guarding her tongue in case she accidentally let Kyle's name slip. Tansy admired the new dish on the bookcase that showed off Fler's shells, asking the inevitable question, 'Where did you get it?'

'The art exhibition after the summer school,' Fler told her, hoping her voice sounded casual, normal. 'One of the students made it.'

She watched in heart-pounding silence as Tansy picked up a shell, inspecting its white underside and purple-inged edge. 'These look good in it,' she said. 'I saw a new jar in the front lounge, too. You've been spending up, haven't you?'

'A bit,' Fler said. 'We're going to be short-staffed in the dining room tonight. Want to help out?'

As soon as she asked, she wondered if she ought to have managed somehow. Suppose the kitchen staff or the waitress said something about the lecturer who had stayed on after the school, helping out round the place?

It didn't happen. The next day was Tansy's last. Fler went to church, but Tansy sleepily declined. When Fler got back, though, she was up and dressed, standing at the door with a peculiarly tense look on her face.

Fler gave her a puzzled frown. 'Is something wrong?'

'No.' She followed her mother into their sitting-room and closed the door. Then she burst out, 'Why didn't you tell me Kyle was here?'

Fler sank down on the sofa. 'How did you find out?'

'His name's in the register. Someone phoned and asked if they'd left something in their room last week. I looked back to see what room they'd been in, because they didn't remember. Kyle's name was there. *Why didn't you tell me?*'

'I thought it might upset you.'

'He was supposed to be at the dig!'

Fler opened her mouth to say, 'I know.' But changed it hastily to, 'Was that why you went on it?'

Tansy flushed, making Fler's heart ache for her. She flung herself down on one of the armchairs opposite the sofa and picked at the upholstery with a fingernail. 'What if it was?' she muttered, not looking at Fler.

Feeling her way delicately, Fler said, 'Darling, it's a bit pointless to keep…pursuing a man who doesn't want you.'

'It's not that! He just thinks I'm too young to—to make a commitment.'

'How do you know?'

'He said so!' Tansy looked up defiantly.

'That he wants you? Or that you're too young?' As Tansy didn't answer, Fler said, 'If he wants you, why didn't he go on the dig instead of coming here?'

'He probably thought I'd be here!' Tansy's face blazed with sudden hope. She laughed. 'Oh, that's it! Poor Kyle. He waited until the end of term, holiday time so I wasn't one of his students any more. He came here to be with me, and I was down in the South Island because I wanted to be with him! Oh, what a waste!'

Fler felt stunned. 'Tansy, I don't think that's——'

She paused. Was her rejection, her disbelief, based on fact or on her own feelings, her own hopes? But Kyle, surely, had been genuinely surprised, even horrified when he saw her that first day. And he couldn't have expected not to see her if he'd deliberately tracked down Tansy at home.

'Tansy,' she tried again. 'I don't think he knew that you live here.'

'Of course he did!'

'Surely if he was leading the dig, he knew that you had your name down for it?'

A faint flicker of uncertainty soon disappeared. 'I don't suppose he looked properly. It would be just a list.'

Fler shut her eyes. When she opened them Tansy was on her feet. 'I know you meant it for the best,' she said, 'but I wish you'd told me. He even stayed an extra week, didn't he? I suppose he was hoping I might come back early. I almost did, too. If only I'd known...'

Fler stood up, too. 'That wasn't the reason,' she said. She recalled him standing by the desk as she spoke to Tansy, the tenseness in him as he said, 'Don't tell her I'm here.'

Tansy said, 'Of course it was.'

Fler shook her head. 'I hurt myself. He thought it was his fault and he stayed to help out.'

Tansy's mouth opened with surprise. Then she said, 'It was an excuse.'

'I don't think so. And I think that he came here to avoid going on the dig with you. Tansy, you have to be realistic about this. At the hospital, after you...took those pills, he told me to get you off his back.'

Tansy went white. Her throat worked, her eyes filling with tears.

Fler's throat felt raw and painful. 'I'm *sorry*, darling. You have to accept that he doesn't want you.'

She made to go to her daughter, to put her arms around her.

Tansy pushed her away. 'Why are you saying these things to me? I thought you loved me!'

Shaken, Fler said, 'I do! More than anyone in the world. It won't do you any good to break your heart over a man who...who isn't interested any more.'

'You don't know what you're talking about!' Tansy said haughtily, the tears momentarily at bay.

'Oh, *Tansy*!' Fler's patience snapped. 'If he really wanted you, what was he doing kissing *me*?'

There was a profound, sickening silence. I shouldn't have said that, Fler thought. Oh, God, she prayed, what will I do now?

Tansy's face looked sallow, her eyes blank with shock. 'What are you talking about?' she said finally.

Fler swallowed. She felt exactly as she had when Tansy was two and Fler had accidentally closed a door on her small fat fingers. 'I don't want to hurt you,' she said.

'You're a liar,' Tansy said flatly.

Fler winced. 'You know very well I'm not.'

'Yes, you are.' Tansy's voice rose. 'I don't know why you want to do this to me, but you're lying.'

Keep your temper, Fler reminded herself. She was torn between anger and pity and a desperate desire to gather her daughter into her arms and comfort her as if she were still a baby. 'I'm not trying to do anything to you——'

'You want him yourself!' Tansy said wonderingly. 'That's what this is about. You think he——'

'That's *not* what this is about!'

The life had come back into Tansy's eyes. They glittered. 'You do!' she said. 'You're in love with Kyle! You can't deny it, can you?'

Fatally, Fler could feel the blood burning in her cheeks. 'That's not the point,' she said.

'Of course it is!' Tansy was looking at her like some stranger, her eyes brilliant, hostile. 'That's what it is. You're jealous!'

'I am not jealous!' But somewhere deep inside her an insidious whisper was saying, Maybe it's true.

'Why should he want *you*?' Tansy asked cruelly. 'You're *years* older than he is!'

'And you're younger!' Fler snapped. 'The age-gap is bigger between you and him than between him and me!'

Tansy blinked. 'It's more natural that way,' she said. 'It's nothing for a man to be older.'

How amazingly conservative the young are, Fler thought, almost tempted to laugh.

Perhaps Tansy noticed. Young people hated to be laughed at, too. Her eyes narrowing, she said, 'You'll never take him away from *me*. You're no good at holding a man, anyway. You couldn't hold Daddy, and you were younger, then.'

Tempted to slap her, Fler clenched her hands rigidly at her sides. 'What happened between your father and

me is none of your business. And it also has nothing to
do with this. I'm trying to save you from getting hurt
again——'

'You've got a funny way of doing it! How *could* you
go behind my back like that?'

'I didn't do anything of the sort!'

'You never mentioned Kyle in your letters.'

'There didn't seem any point——'

'Hah! I suppose not, when you were batting your eye-
lashes at him for all you were worth, hoping to interest
him in you. Making a fool of yourself. It's *pathetic*, at
your age!'

'I didn't do anything of the kind! As a matter of fact
I didn't need to!'

What was she doing? Having a fight over a man with
her daughter? This had to stop.

'If he did kiss you,' Tansy sneered, 'it was probably
because he was sorry for you! Did you just pretend to
hurt yourself, so he'd have to pick you up and comfort
you? What did you do? Sprain an ankle? I bet it's perfectly all right now!'

Fler took a deep breath. 'You're upset right now. Why
don't we talk about it in the morning?'

'There's nothing more to talk about,' Tansy said. 'I
don't know if I'll ever want to speak to you again! I
don't think I ever want to *see* you again!'

She stalked off to her room and slammed the door.

Fler tried to see some humour in the dramatic exit
line, and failed. She was horribly afraid that her relationship with Tansy had suffered some irreparable
damage. And all over a man.

She sat down on the sofa, trembling with reaction.

Had she made a fool of herself over Kyle? She knew
she hadn't, as Tansy had suggested, run after him. But
she'd been all too ready to yield to his careful pursuit.

And that was what it had been, she thought, looking back. Once she'd accused him of playing Tansy like a fish. Had he done that with her, too? He'd certainly got under her defences in less than four weeks.

Part of her said, No, it wasn't like that. But that was how Tansy felt, too. Tansy was convinced that he loved her. And no matter how he felt now, maybe once he had wanted Tansy, and pursued her with the same deceptive gentleness.

She'd said that, Fler recalled. 'He was so gentle with me, always.' Smiling secretly, tenderly.

Fler put her hands over her face. No man was worth losing her daughter. Certainly not a man who was capable of deliberately setting out to seduce them both.

Thank God that at least he hadn't got that far with her.

# CHAPTER TEN

TANSY left that afternoon, during the short journey to the bus stop stiffly answering when she was spoken to and refusing to meet Fler's eyes.

'Darling,' Fler said as the passengers began to board, 'please promise me you won't do anything silly.'

Tansy's clear, hostile eyes met hers. 'You can talk.'

Maybe she had a point there, Fler conceded. What could be sillier than falling in love with your daughter's ex-lover? 'I mean——'

'I know what you mean.' Tansy smiled thinly. 'No more pills. What do you care, anyway?'

Fler's already precarious patience snapped. 'Oh, Tansy! Don't be *ridiculous*! You know how much I care.'

'I have to get on the bus,' Tansy said distantly. 'Goodbye.'

She avoided Fler's kiss and took her place in the line, presenting her ticket to the driver. Helplessly, Fler watched her climb on board. She chose a seat on the far side of the aisle and disappeared from view.

Fler worried all the way home. Tansy seemed convinced that Kyle was only waiting for her return to take up their relationship where they'd left off. But he'd certainly given no indication in that direction to Fler.

Would he have, though, if he was toying with the idea of an affair with Tansy's mother? She made herself examine the idea that maybe he was playing them off against each other. He had, after all, been the one to suggest the ban on talking about Tansy for the duration of his stay.

But surely he couldn't have faked that thunderstruck reaction to Fler's presence, the blank look when she'd told him Tansy wasn't at Manaaki.

And if he rebuffed her again, what might Tansy do?

No more pills, she'd said with mockery in her voice. Had it been a promise, or just an acknowledgement of her mother's concern?

Fler frowned. She felt cold. She should never have allowed Tansy to return to Auckland.

More sanely, she acknowledged that nothing could have persuaded Tansy to stay home. She'd arranged to share another flat with two of her former flatmates and someone called Pat whom she'd met on the dig. At least the two who'd lived with her last year might know the signs to watch for next time.

There won't be a next time, Fler tried to reassure herself. She wouldn't do it again. She'd said so after the last time.

But the nagging fear wouldn't go away. For the rest of that day and all of the next she was absentminded with worry.

She had to do something. On Monday evening she looked up the register and found that Kyle had written in his home phone number when he signed it. She scribbled it on a piece of paper, took it into her bedroom and sat on the bed, alternately looking at the piece of paper and the telephone, rehearsing what she could say.

Finally she picked up the receiver and dialled, half hoping there would be no answer.

When Kyle's decisive 'Hello?' came on the line, for a moment she couldn't speak. The terrible thought flitted through her mind that she had only made Tansy an excuse for the exquisite pleasure of hearing his voice.

'Hello?' he said again. 'Kyle Ranburn speaking.'

'Kyle,' she said. 'It's Fler. Fler Daniels.'

It was his turn to be silent. Then he said, 'I only know one Fler. How are you?' He made the conventional query sound almost urgent, as though he really needed to know.

'All right,' she said, but her voice wavered, the warmth and concern that emanated from him even through the cold medium of the telephone bringing a silly impulse to cry.

'What's the matter?' he asked instantly, sharply. 'You're *not* all right. Are you?'

'Yes, but——' She swallowed. 'It's Tansy.'

'Tansy.' His voice cooled noticeably. 'What's she done now?'

'Nothing. She's back in Auckland. I think...she seems to think...well, that you and she are still...that you might get together again.'

He was silent for so long this time that she said, 'Are you there?'

'Yes. Did you phone to warn me?'

That sounded as though Tansy was some kind of dangerous animal on the loose. 'I phoned to ask you...well...not to hurt her.'

'Would you like to spell that out?' he asked. His voice was definitely cold now.

Floundering, she tried to explain. 'She thinks you came here to see her.'

Kyle made an exasperated, breathy sound. 'She couldn't be further wrong, actually.'

'I tried to tell her that. She wouldn't listen.'

Rather curtly, he asked, 'What am I supposed to do about it, Fler?'

She didn't know. 'I just don't want her hurt. I don't want another call to the hospital in the middle of the night. Can't you...?'

'What? Take her to bed and give her what she thinks she wants? Ask her to marry me, perhaps? Or make her my mistress? Take your pick, Fler. Which do you want me to do?'

The gentle concern was quite gone now. The voice was that of a hard, angry stranger.

'I'm sorry,' she said. 'I shouldn't have bothered you.'

She put down the handpiece and sat staring blankly at the wall. That had been a stupid idea. She flipped open the index that sat beside the telephone and dialled the number of Tansy's new flat. Thank heaven she'd written it down before Tansy got into a rage with her.

A masculine voice answered. 'Pat here.'

Pat was a boy? She'd assumed another female flatmate. 'Is Tansy there?' she asked. 'It's her mother.'

Maybe she shouldn't have said who it was. Suppose Tansy had told her flatmates she wouldn't answer calls from her mother?

But Pat said cheerfully, 'Hang on a minute. I'll get her.'

Tansy sounded subdued and wary. 'What do you want?'

What did she want? Fler said, 'Just to make sure you got there safely.'

With slight long-suffering, Tansy said, 'Of course I did. What did you think? That I'd be mugged between the bus stop and the flat?'

'Well, I hoped not.' To fill the slight pause that ensued, Fler added, 'I didn't realise your new flatmate was male. I thought Pat would be a girl.'

'Is it a problem?' Tansy asked defensively.

'Not at all.' Determinedly cheerful and neutral. 'He sounds nice.'

'He's OK.'

'Well...look after yourself, darling. I love you.'

She waited, her teeth sunk into her lower lip, tears stinging her eyes. Then, along the wire came Tansy's muttered, 'I love you too, Mum. Goodnight.'

Her heart soaring with relief, Fler put down the phone. Things might be a bit rocky, but the lines of communication were open. She hadn't lost Tansy.

She was in the bathroom brushing her teeth when the phone rang. Hastily she rinsed her mouth out and snatched up a towel as she ran to answer it.

Kyle's voice said, 'Fler, we have to talk.'

'I just tried——'

'Not on the phone. It's going to be hard for me to get away for a while, but I will if I have to. Term's just beginning and I'm up to my ears. Is there any chance you can come down to Auckland soon?'

She'd make one. Bookings had dwindled to a trickle by now. 'Yes,' she said, not giving herself a chance to back down. 'What about next weekend? Does that suit you?'

'Thank you. Saturday? Sunday?'

'Saturday afternoon. I could get away after lunch if I can clear it with Rae. I'll stay overnight and come back Sunday.'

'Good. Where will you be staying? Can I pick you up? We could have dinner.'

'No. I'll meet you.' She'd have to find a motel. Once or twice she'd stayed at Tansy's flat last year, but the new one might not have a spare bed or sofa, and besides, it would be difficult meeting Kyle from there. Tansy would want to know where she was going.

He mentioned a restaurant that he said was easy to find. 'I'll book us a table. Seven-thirty suit you?'

She said it was fine, and they politely bade each other goodnight. Afterwards Fler sat staring into space, her mind oddly blank. Was this a date? A discussion? What?

'We have to talk', he'd said. After she'd phoned him about Tansy. A discussion. Forget the warm flooding of desire that had surged through her body at the sound of his voice, and the strange breathless anticipation at the very thought of seeing him again. Her concern was with Tansy. That was what this meeting was all about.

Kyle was standing outside the restaurant, looking casually elegant in dark trousers and a pale apricot shirt without a tie. Coming up to him, she said, 'Am I late? I'm sorry, I had trouble finding a parking space for the car.'

'I was early,' he said. 'I didn't want you to be hanging about waiting.'

The restaurant was crowded, and he said, 'Last time I came here it didn't seem quite so public. I think they've crammed in some extra tables since then. Well . . . let's enjoy our meal, anyway.'

Taking that to mean that he didn't want to broach the subject of Tansy yet, Fler nodded and bent her head to the menu.

She was disconcerted to find that he had lost none of his magnetism for her. Even while she studied the list of dishes before her, she was acutely aware of his every movement, the dark curve of his lashes as he looked down at his own menu, the lean grace of the fingers that held it, the exact angle of his head as he turned the page.

They ordered, and he asked her about Rae and the other staff he had got to know. And whether the possum had ever reappeared.

'No,' she said, 'thank goodness. I guess you frightened him off.'

'Me? I wasn't the one casting aspersions on his character and threatening to have him exterminated.'

'I didn't threaten!'

'You said you'd have him killed.'

'That was next morning.' She had a sudden vivid memory of Kyle standing outside her window in the morning sun, calling her a softie. 'What I said was that I'd hate to have to do it. And anyway, he was gone by then.'

Kyle was smiling rather absently, even though he was looking straight at her. Why did she *know* in her bones that he was seeing her framed in her bedroom window, her hair still tousled from sleep?

'Yes, you're right,' he said suddenly. 'It was next morning, but how do you know he wasn't still within earshot?'

This was an idiotic conversation. Yet the blood was singing in her veins, a bubble of laughter threatening to escape her throat. 'We're crazy!' she told him.

His smile deepened, and the light in his eyes made her heart skip a beat in a way it hadn't since she was eighteen years old and madly in love with Rick. 'I don't know about you,' he said quite seriously, 'but I know I am.'

The waiter brought their soup, and she tore her gaze away from Kyle's. This wasn't what she was here for, she reminded herself. This can't be *allowed* to happen.

But it was happening, and it went on happening all through the meal, while they ate their soup and main courses and consulted on desserts and decided against any. Until Kyle said, 'I made a mistake. This is no place for a serious discussion. Fler, will you come back to my place?'

She hesitated, trying to still the singing in her veins, and he said, 'Unless you prefer to go to wherever you're staying.'

'A motel,' she said, and they looked at each other and then, with mutual dry humour, said in unison, 'No!'

'My place,' Kyle said. 'I promise you this is not a ploy to lure you to my den. Coffee here, or wait until we get there?'

The waiter hovered, and Fler said, 'Whatever you prefer.' She was suddenly nervous, and not sure why. She was old enough not to go all dewy-eyed and palpitating at the idea of going to a man's flat, for heaven's sake. Besides, he'd made it clear he had no romantic intentions, hadn't he?

He eyed her thoughtfully and ordered two coffees. 'We can have more later, if you like.'

She drank it down quite quickly, and then he walked her to her car and said, 'I'll go slowly so you can follow. It's not far.'

He lived in a third-floor apartment in a renovated building five minutes from the university. She looked about at the spacious, high-ceilinged room with a large oriental rug on the floor and several deep comfortable chairs grouped about a low, round table. 'Sit down,' Kyle said and, going to a corner table, he lifted the receiver off the telephone that stood there. 'I don't want to be interrupted,' he explained at her questioning glance. 'Can I get you anything?' he offered. 'More coffee? I have some Irish cream, or Drambuie.'

They'd shared a carafe of wine with their meal, but she'd drunk sparingly. 'Thank you. I'll have a glass of Irish cream.'

'Sit down while I get it.'

She took one of the chairs, sinking into its soft blue velvet upholstery. Each was a different colour, picking up the colours of the carpet. Midnight-blue, moss-green, deep crimson and rich old gold.

On the wall facing her was a large painting. She was trying to figure out its subject when Kyle returned with two liqueur glasses filled with pale coffee-coloured liquid.

'Do you like it?' he asked, nodding towards the painting as he sat down opposite her.

'I haven't decided yet,' Fler said cautiously. 'I suppose the last question I should ask is, what is it?'

Kyle laughed. 'It's called *Passion Flowers* if that's any help.'

Fler sipped at her drink and returned her gaze to the painting. 'Maybe.' It had streaks and whorls of purple, white and red. She had the feeling that if she gazed at it for a long time she might find herself inexorably drawn into the picture, unable to escape.

Mentally she shook herself, experiencing a strange reluctance to get to the point of this meeting. But when she'd drained her glass and he offered more, she shook her head firmly. 'No, thank you. You said you want to talk.'

'Yes.' Kyle took her glass and placed it carefully beside his on the round table. He went back to his seat and for a few moments sat leaning forward with his hands loosely clasped, frowning down at them. Then he looked up and said, 'I'm going to ask you to do something, please.'

'What?'

'Just listen. Let me talk, and try to listen with an open mind until I've finished. After that, you can say what you like, ask any questions you want to.'

Fler nodded.

'Thank you,' Kyle said formally. He seemed to gather his thoughts, his gaze again on his hands. 'Last year,' he said, 'about this time last year, I went to a party given by a friend of mine who also works at the university. He's older than me, his children are from eighteen to about thirty years old. Some of their friends were invited, too. I met this young woman.' He looked up, holding Fler's gaze. 'Tansy.'

Fler felt her muscles tighten with tension.

'We got talking. It started with a discussion of a painting that my friend had on the wall. She seemed to know something about art.'

'She took art history in her last year at school.'

Kyle nodded. 'As you know, I have an amateur interest, too. We got on quite well.'

So far what he said agreed with what Tansy had written in letters about their meeting.

I met this real neat guy at a party. He knows a lot about paintings. We talked for hours.

'That was quite early in the evening. Later we bumped into each other again and had another brief chat. When I was about to leave she was trying to phone a taxi in the hall. She was having some trouble getting through. I asked her where she lived, and as it was on my way I offered her a lift.'

Kyle paused, pushing back his hair off his forehead. A frown reappeared between his brows. 'If I'd known then . . .' He shook his head. 'Anyway, on the way home I remembered I had been invited to an exhibition of contemporary New Zealand art opening the following day. I hadn't made up my mind whether to go but I thought she'd enjoy it. We hadn't exchanged any personal information, but I gathered she'd only been in Auckland for a short time. I don't know why it didn't occur to me she was a student, except that she'd dressed herself up to look older than she was. And she was wearing quite a lot of make-up that night. She looked . . . very sophisticated.'

'And you were . . . attracted.'

He chewed his lip, the frown deepening. Slowly, he said, 'Tansy is a pretty girl. And I liked her. She was intelligent—*nice*, good company. We went to the exhibition, and it was an enjoyable afternoon. We had dinner together. Why not? We both seemed to be at a loose end. I asked her that night what she did, and she fudged the answer.'

'What do you mean?'

'By that time I'd told her what my job was. She sort of hedged about, and I got the impression she was unemployed. I didn't press it because I thought she was embarrassed. She said something about having worked around a guest house in her student days.'

Fler's lips opened in surprise, but she didn't utter a word.

'I gathered those days were behind her,' Kyle said. 'When I took her home, she mentioned she'd been given some free tickets to a play she thought I'd like.' He paused again. 'To refuse would have been a direct snub. We went to the play together, and when we parted that evening, it was obvious she expected me to kiss her.'

Fler's mouth was dry. She recalled Tansy asking if she remembered Rick's first kiss. 'And you obliged.'

He looked directly at her. 'I swear to you, I meant it to be a friendly peck. I was surprised—rocked—by her reaction. I extricated myself as best I could without, I hoped, being totally insensitive. Later I told myself I was a reactionary male chauvinist under the skin—put off by a woman taking the initiative. The episode bothered me. It didn't dawn on me for a while that one of the things that worried me was that despite her—eagerness, she was essentially inexperienced. It showed.'

'She was then,' Fler said bitterly.

A spasm of anger tightened his jaw. 'You promised,' he reminded her.

Fler clamped her mouth shut.

'That's when I began to suspect she was younger than I'd imagined. About a week later I came across her at the university, and realised she was a student. And a mere teenager. It gave me a jolt, but I thought there'd been no harm done, and forgot about it. Until she turned up in my class. She'd changed her course.'

'Yes,' Fler said. 'I know.' What she had not known until much later was that Kyle Ranburn was the lecturer for Tansy's new subject.

'She seemed inclined to linger after class, and... I'm not particularly formal with my students, but Tansy's attitude was giving a wrong impression to the others about our previous...acquaintanceship. Eventually I had to say something.' Again Kyle pushed his hair back, frowning. 'She seemed to take it well, said she was sorry and she understood.' He shook his head. 'In class she stopped saying anything at all. But outside she began waylaying me at every opportunity. Any transparent excuse would do. She hadn't understood something I'd said, could I just take a minute to explain? She couldn't read her notes, what was the name of the book I'd recommended, again? She was anxious about her essay, the library book she needed was out on loan until next week. Anything. It wasn't hard to guess she had a full-blown crush on me.' He glanced up, looking embarrassed.

'It can't have been the first time,' Fler suggested.

Kyle shook his head. 'Usually it's easily handled. I'd never met anyone as persistent as Tansy. I tried being gentle at first.'

*'He was so gentle with me, always.'*

'It made no difference,' he said wearily. 'I tried being firm. She smiled at me sunnily and said she knew it was difficult for me, she would be good. For a while I thought I'd succeeded in getting through to her. Then she started writing me letters, putting them in with her written work. I tore them up, told her to stop. One day when I was about to start a lecture I found an envelope on the lectern, her writing on it. She was in the front row, with this eager, expectant smile on her face.'

He glanced at Fler. 'You're going to hate this.'

She swallowed, staring back at him. His face was pale.

Kyle said, 'I'd had enough. I couldn't see an end to it unless I did something drastic. I picked it up, looked at Tansy again so she'd be in no doubt that I knew who it was from. Then I deliberately tore up the letter without opening it, and threw the pieces in the wastebasket. In front of the whole class. I didn't look at her once for the rest of the lecture. I couldn't.' His face twisted with pain. 'That was the night she phoned me at home here and said she'd taken those pills.'

Fler was sitting perfectly still, but hot tears welled into her eyes and scalded down her cheeks.

'Oh, *God*, Fler, I'm so sorry!' He left his chair and knelt at her side, first grabbing her hands in a hard clasp, then putting his arms about her, pulling her head on to his shoulder.

For a few seconds she let him hold her, then she pulled back, wiping the back of her hand across her eyes, scrabbling in the bag at her side for a handkerchief.

Kyle stood up and waited. When she had wiped away the tears, he said quietly, 'I was at the end of my tether. By the time I spoke to you at the hospital, I'd got past the guilty stage, I was bloody angry. Partly in reaction at the fright I'd got when I thought she might actually die. But for Tansy's sake as well as mine, I hoped I could persuade you to get her some professional help.'

Fler took a shaky breath. 'But she was all right afterwards,' she protested. 'She told me she knew she'd been silly, that she wouldn't do it again.'

'Yes, she told me that, too. Something I said to her must have penetrated—about childish ways of getting attention. She assured me she was going to grow up, be adult from now on.'

'She said that to me, too,' Fler murmured.

'I hoped it meant that her teenage infatuation had worn itself out. So I told her I was glad to hear it, and wished her well.' He thrust his hands into his pockets, stared at the carpet. 'I thought it was over. Then just before the year's end, she stopped me one day and said something enigmatic about how "we" wouldn't have to pretend for much longer. That was all. She smiled at me and went on her way. But it brought me out in a cold sweat, and then I saw her name on the list of students who'd volunteered for the archeology group I was supposed to be leading in the holidays.'

'I know about that,' she reminded him. 'You swapped.'

'Yes. I talked Hathaway into it, and insisted on keeping the change secret. He was keen enough, though he thought I was crazy. After it was all arranged I began to wonder if I was, too. Maybe I was being paranoid. But I'm glad now that I did the swap. Otherwise I'd never have gone to Manaaki. Never have met *you* again.'

# CHAPTER ELEVEN

'*ME?*'

Kyle shifted on his feet, planting them slightly apart on the floor, his hands still in his pockets. 'You must know by now,' he said, 'that I'm in love with you.'

Fler stared at him blankly. For an absurd moment all she could think of was that she must look awful, her eyes reddened and her face probably pale, her mouth slightly agape with surprise.

And yet, why surprise? She'd acknowledged to herself that in four weeks she had fallen in love with Kyle. Why shouldn't he feel the same way?

Because...

Her voice husky and uneven, she asked, 'Did you ever make love to Tansy?'

His expression went rigid. 'No.'

'You said she's pretty, you liked her company.'

He sighed. 'Fler, remember that bowl that I bought for you?'

'Yes,' Fler said uncertainly.

'There were other pieces that were more elaborate, probably better executed, certainly more noticeable, weren't there?'

'Yes.'

'You did appreciate, even admire some of the other work?'

'Of course.'

'But there was only that one you could hardly bear to leave behind. I saw how you regretted not buying it.'

And so he'd bought it for her.

He said, 'Tansy was like those others, Fler. Someone I liked but didn't have any burning need to see again, to have in my life. Surely you must have had men friends that you feel like that about?'

Not many, but there had been one or two whose company she'd enjoyed, yet who failed to stir her senses to any degree. 'Yes,' she acknowledged.

'Then you know what I'm talking about.'

'I suppose I do,' she said slowly. She was trying to assimilate all that he had told her, trying not to let the rest of it be overwhelmed by the single, final, heart-stopping statement that Kyle was in love with her.

She searched for evidence of it in his face, but he seemed to have closed down, his features rigidly controlled.

'Any more questions?' he asked rather harshly.

Fler moistened her lips. He'd said she could ask what she wanted to once he'd finished. 'Why didn't you tell me all this before?'

His look held impatience now. 'I tried to give you the gist that day at the hospital, but you didn't want to hear it. At Manaaki, before I left, I certainly intended to tell you the whole story. You made it clear that it wasn't the right time. When I came home I tried writing to you. On paper it looked cold and, I have to confess, unlikely. I told myself to forget it, the whole thing was too complicated. But that wasn't so easy. I knew I had to see you again. And then you phoned.'

'You didn't exactly sound as though you were pleased to hear from me.'

'Not when I realised that you'd contacted me solely on Tansy's behalf. I'd hoped . . .' He gestured with one hand. 'But obviously we had to clear the air about her. I hope I've done that tonight.'

Fler moved her hands, found they were shaking, and clasped them in her lap. 'Tansy said ... implied ...' what *had* Tansy said exactly? It was difficult now to recall her actual words '... that you were lovers.'

Kyle took a deep breath. 'It isn't true, Fler. You have to believe me!'

She looked at his face, searched his eyes, darkened and steady. 'I believe you,' she said.

He let out the breath he'd been holding. 'Thank heaven!' Then, his eyes alight suddenly, he swooped and pulled her out of the chair and into his arms. 'Thank heaven,' he said again, his lips moving against her hair, and then his hand found her chin and raised her head, and his mouth came down on hers.

It was a fairly devastating kiss, not gentle at all, but passionate, seeking, compelling. After a second or two he wrapped both arms about her, and hers instinctively slid about his neck, her body arching into his hard embrace, her head tilting back under the hungry persuasion of his mouth.

He lifted his mouth, his hands coming up to cradle her head while he looked down at her flushed face, his eyes brilliant with desire. 'I've been wanting to do that forever,' he muttered, and then kissed her mouth again, and her cheek, and trailed hot kisses down the line of her throat, flicking his tongue into the shallow depression at its base. His hands smoothed the skin of her neck, warmed the skin of her shoulders inside her blouse, moving down.

Her blouse stopped him, and he impatiently pulled open a couple of buttons, settled a warm palm on her breast over the satin and lace of her bra, and kissed her again.

His tongue traced the line of her upper lip, and his thumb was moving on the firm swell above the low-cut lace of her bra. Then it was dipping under the lace, gently squeezing the eager, hardening centre against the edge of his hand that was stroking the satin-covered curve.

Her mouth parted on a quick breath, and he slid his tongue inside and began an erotic foray that made her tremble with delight.

She felt the answering tremor that shook his body, and she pressed against him, her mouth fully open to him now, her eyes tightly closed so that her whole attention was concentrated on the giving and receiving of this incredible pleasure that made her body feel weightless, floating, and her ears buzz, shutting out all sound except Kyle's quickened breathing.

He made an impatient little sound and fumbled at the rest of her buttons, tearing them open. For a moment their bodies parted, glazed eyes staring at each other, and then he pushed back her blouse and was touching her bare skin, his hands running from her waist to her ribcage, his fingers splaying on her midriff, then delicately stroking over the thin white fabric that covered her breasts. 'This is pretty,' he said, 'but I'll bet what's underneath is even prettier.'

She knew her figure was still good, her breasts firm and full, but a tiny shiver of anxiety assailed her as he moved his hands behind her and began to fumble with the clasp. She'd had a child; her body wasn't that of a young girl. She wanted him to find her beautiful, and dreaded his disappointment.

Her hands rested on his chest, almost as if to stop him, and he looked at her enquiringly.

Then the doorbell went, a long, insistent, intrusive electric buzz.

Fler froze. Kyle's head jerked up, and he said something explosive and extremely rude.

Fler pulled away from him, but he hauled her back into his arms and said tensely, 'Ignore it.'

His lips descended again on hers, his hand sliding the blouse off her shoulder, but this time the buzzing in her ears wasn't passion. The sound went on and on until Kyle tore away his mouth and cursed again.

'It must be important,' she said. 'You'd better answer it.' She straightened her blouse and began doing up buttons. 'A mirror?' she said, thinking how she must look, untidy and flushed and in no state to be seen by anyone.

'The bedroom's through there,' he said, indicating a door. 'I'll get rid of whoever it is as quietly as I can.'

As he strode towards the small entrance hall, Fler grabbed up her bag and fled to the bedroom. The mirror over a long dressing-table showed her eyes still darkened with passion, cheeks dusky rose, her mouth denuded of lipstick, but red and full, her hair tousled out of its usual neat style.

Her fingers stilled as she stared. She didn't remember ever seeing herself like this, looking so alive and vibrant—so loved.

Kyle's voice in the hall said something sharp. Her fingers were unsteady. She gave up on the buttons, picked up a comb that lay on the dressing-table and hastily dragged it through her hair.

And quite clearly through the door that was several inches ajar, she heard Tansy's voice in the next room say, 'I know she's here. I saw her car outside.'

Shock held her immobile, jolted through her body like a bolt of electricity. Kyle's voice said, 'If you'd tell me what the problem is, Tansy——' and then, sharply, 'No, you can't go in there!'

But although he was right behind her, he was too late. Tansy had thrust open the door. As Fler turned her head in stunned disbelief, the girl gave a pathetic, mewing little cry, staring at her mother standing in Kyle's bedroom with her blouse still half unbuttoned, his comb in her hand and the imprint of his kisses unmistakably on her mouth.

For a timeless moment they seemed locked in a tableau. Kyle's expression was tight and furious. Fler knew that hers was shocked, flustered and probably guilty. And as she watched, all the colour drained from Tansy's horrified face, leaving it white and empty.

Fler said sharply, '*Kyle*! She's going to faint!'

Instinctively he put a hand on Tansy's shoulder, even as Fler dropped the comb and moved towards her daughter.

But Tansy backed from her, shaking off Kyle's hand, moving into the lounge, away from them. 'I'm not going to faint,' she said, as some of the colour came back into her cheeks. 'Don't touch me—either of you!' Her eyes, wounded and tragic, went from Kyle to Fler. 'How could you?' A dry sob heaved at her slim shoulders. 'How could you both do this to me?'

Fler said quickly, 'Tansy, it isn't what you think——'

Kyle, looking at Fler, said, 'Isn't it?'

Angrily, Fler met his gaze, finding in it an anger of his own that more than matched hers.

Couldn't he see that Tansy was *hurting*? She and Kyle were adults, they could sort out their problems later. But Tansy had just suffered a major shock. And Kyle seemed bent on making it worse.

Kyle said, 'What are you doing here, Tansy?'

Tansy's eyes flickered away from the hard eyes that matched his tone. 'I told you, I wanted to see my mother.'

His gaze flicked to Fler. 'You told her,' he suggested sardonically, 'that you were going to meet me tonight?'

'No.' She in turn looked at her daughter. 'How did you know I was here?'

'I *guessed*!' Her tone dared Fler to disbelieve her.

'After you saw her car,' Kyle said flatly. 'You couldn't possibly have known beforehand. Neither of us had planned to come back here.'

Fler experienced the briefest flicker of doubt. He hadn't...?

Tansy said, 'Hah!'

'How long,' Kyle enquired coldly, 'have you been staking out my apartment?'

'What makes you think I have?' She tried valiantly to meet his eyes, but his grim mouth and steady gaze defeated her. 'I thought you were out,' she said.

His brows drew together. 'The lights were on.'

'Before!' Tansy said in goaded tones. 'I thought you were out, because...'

'Because I wasn't answering the phone. I was, earlier. When we came in I took it off the hook.'

'So you wouldn't be disturbed?' Tansy cried, almost triumphantly. Her eyes went from him to her mother and back. Fler was shaken by the expression in them.

Kyle said evenly, 'That's right. Because lately I've been getting a lot of nuisance calls.' He paused. 'It was you, wasn't it? Phoning and then hanging up when I answered.'

Fler felt sick.

'What if it was?' Tansy asked. 'All I wanted...'

'Yes?' Kyle said. 'What did you want, Tansy?' His voice was implacable, cold.

Fler saw Tansy flinch. 'Kyle,' she said. 'Stop it, *please*!'

'No,' he said. 'You didn't think I was out, did you, Tansy? You thought I was here with someone, and you wanted to—what? Spy on us?'

Tansy flushed now, a brilliant pink. 'I wouldn't have come in,' she said, 'only when I saw her car——' Her accusing gaze swept to Fler, shocking her anew. Fler might have been a stranger, one that Tansy actively disliked.

Fler said urgently, 'Tansy, we'd been out to dinner—to talk about *you*! And I went into his room to tidy myself, comb my hair...'

Kyle cast her a glance almost of contempt. 'You're not helping, Fler.'

'Do you think *you* are?' she flared at him. 'Tansy, I am not having an affair with Kyle!'

His eyebrows shot up, and he cast her a sardonic look which she ignored, concentrating her attention on Tansy. 'Have I ever lied to you?' she asked gently.

Tansy swallowed, gave a faint, reluctant shake of her head.

Kyle said coolly, 'That doesn't mean I wouldn't like to make love to your mother. As a matter of fact I have every intention of doing so one day.'

'Kyle!' Fler protested as Tansy seemed to shrink into herself, stricken. That was gratuitous cruelty. Couldn't he see what he was doing?

'This has gone far enough,' he said. 'It's time we got a few things out in the open. Your mother,' he said to Tansy, 'was under the impression that you and I had been sleeping together.'

Tansy was shaking. Fler whispered, 'Kyle!'

She made to cross the room to her daughter, but Tansy said, 'No! Keep away from me!' She had her arms wrapped about herself now, and was looking at Kyle with something like fear lurking behind the defiance in her eyes.

'I told her,' he said, 'that wasn't true.'

For a moment Fler thought Tansy wasn't going to react at all. Then her eyes swivelled to her mother. She said, and her tone sounded wounded, 'You *believed* him?'

Feeling treacherous, Fler moistened dry lips, her heart wrenched at the accusing look of betrayal in Tansy's eyes.

Kyle said, 'Yes, she believed me. Now I want *you* to tell her.'

Tansy looked back at him, her mouth parting, moving soundlessly. Finally she whispered, 'I…c-can't do that.'

Kyle's patience snapped. He took two strides and caught Tansy's shoulders in a fierce grip. She gave a gasp of fright, her eyes widening on the white rage in his face, and then Fler was there, tearing at his hands. '*Don't you touch her*! Let her *go*, Kyle!'

She thumped at his chest with a fist, pushing him further away as he released his grip, and then turned as Tansy stumbled into her arms, crying uncontrollably.

She stroked Tansy's hair, murmured soothingly to her, rocked her, while Kyle stood by silently emanating frustration and fury.

When the sobs that wracked Tansy's slight body quieted, Fler said, 'Shh, it's all right. I'll take you home, now. You can stay with me tonight. OK?'

Tansy nodded against her shoulder. Kyle's mouth twisted in what was almost a sneer. Over Tansy's head, Fler said quietly to him, 'Would you get my bag, please?'

'Get it yourself.'

She blinked at the blatant discourtesy. Then she drew her gaze away from the cold anger in his and eased Tansy into the chair. 'I'll be back in a minute,' she said. And to Kyle, 'Don't touch her.'

'I have no such intention,' he assured her, and followed her into the bedroom, closing the door behind him as she took her bag from the dressing-table.

Fler stiffened, turning to face him. 'What do you want?'

'You,' he said. 'This.' And he came to her and pulled her to him and brought his mouth down on hers with brief, stormy passion.

She'd hardly begun to fight him before he stepped away from her, breathing hard. 'Call me before you go back home,' he said. '*Please*! You know we have things to say to each other. One day there'll be a time and a place just for us.'

She was too wrought-up and confused to answer him, and after a moment he opened the door for her and let her walk back into the other room. Tansy was curled in the chair, her face hidden in the crook of her arm, fair hair spreading over the sleeve of her sweatshirt. She looked like a beaten, defenceless child.

'Come on, darling,' Fler urged her, touching her hand.

She got up and obediently walked to the door, her tear-streaked face tired and pale. Kyle opened that door, too. Neither of them looked at him, and Fler was surprised when he came with them to the car, waiting until they had driven off. For all the notice that Tansy took of him, he might not have been there. But Fler couldn't resist a glance in the rear-vision mirror, which showed her Kyle standing on the edge of the kerb with one hand thrust into a pocket, his hair lifting slightly in the night breeze as he stared after the car.

# CHAPTER TWELVE

FLER took Tansy to the motel for the night and tucked her into the spare bed as if she were a little girl again. She'd sort out the extra unexpected guest with the management in the morning.

Surprisingly, Tansy slept soundly and long. Fler lay awake most of the night, her mind over-active, replaying events with relentless monotony.

In the morning Tansy was calm and polite, and over a late breakfast of toast and coffee stubbornly refused any discussion of the previous evening, gazing over Fler's shoulder with an aloof, distant expression when the subject was broached.

'The university has student counsellors, doesn't it?' Fler said.

'What about it?'

'Don't you think it might help you... to talk to someone?'

'No.'

Fler, feeling as though she was trying to talk to a wall, finally said, 'Tansy, putting aside the fact that it happened to be me with Kyle last night, you must realise that continually phoning someone and hanging up, going to his flat at night just to—to find out what he's doing, isn't... sensible behaviour.'

Tansy's cool gaze swivelled to her. 'How did you feel when Daddy was running round with other women?'

Fler felt winded. 'How... who told you that?'

'I'm not stupid. Anyway, *he* told me, himself. He said he wasn't proud of it, and you had every right to be jealous. He said he was wrong for you. You needed a one-woman man.'

'When did he say that?'

Tansy shrugged. 'I was fifteen, I think. *Were* you jealous?'

'Of course. I was his wife, I expected him to be faithful. I know that the divorce hurt you, Tansy. I'm sorry, but I couldn't live that way.'

'I understand. Can't *you* understand how I feel about Kyle?'

Fler felt helpless. 'Yes . . . but that's different.' And at Tansy's scornful glance, 'He made you no promises, Tansy. He...says there was never anything between you.'

Tansy's eyes met hers. 'Does he?'

A small hammer started pounding in Fler's head.

'Well,' Tansy said, 'if that's what he says, you'll just have to decide, won't you? Whether you believe him, or believe me.'

She got up and started clearing the table.

'Tansy——' Fler got up, too, reaching out to touch the girl's arm.

Tansy adroitly avoided it. 'Have you finished with that cup? I'll fix these, if you like, while you check out. It's after ten already, they'll be wanting to get rid of us. Can you drop me back at the flat?'

'Yes, of course,' Fler said. 'We could have lunch together first if you like.'

An absent smile. 'No, thanks. I'm sort of tied up for lunch, anyway.'

The flat door opened before Tansy inserted her key in the lock. A young man, stocky, open-faced, sandy-haired, stood there, a scowl on his face that miraculously disappeared when he saw Tansy. 'Where've you *been*?' he demanded. 'We've been worried sick about you!'

A girl wandering down the passage beyond him, her hair wrapped in a towel, said cheerfully, 'Speak for yourself, Pat! The rest of us were mildly concerned.' But Fler noticed the relief in her expression. 'Hi, Tansy. I'm glad you're here to put him out of his misery. Oh, hello, Mrs Daniels.'

Fler said hello, recognising the girl who had helped her pack after Tansy's suicide bid. The girl disappeared through a doorway, and Tansy said, 'Thanks for bringing me home, Mum. Have a safe trip back.'

Fler hovered but she clearly wasn't going to be asked in. 'Are you sure you're all right?' she asked in a low voice.

Tansy's smile was bland, her eyes innocently surprised. 'I'm fine. You go on home, and don't worry about me.'

Fler was in the car, reluctantly switching on the engine, when a tap on the window made her look up. Lowering it, she looked up into Pat's nice, boyishly handsome face. 'We'll look after her, Mrs Daniels. The girls told me what she did to herself last year. And they *were* worried.' He glanced back at the flat as if to assure himself Tansy wasn't watching. 'She's OK, really. I won't let anything happen to her.'

He looked terribly young and earnest, and it was probably silly to feel reassured. But she smiled at him gratefully and thanked him sincerely before driving off.

\*     \*     \*

'Call me,' Kyle had said. *'Please.'*

*'You'll just have to decide...whether you believe him, or believe me.'*

Tansy had never been an untruthful child. Apart from the odd fib when she was very young, Fler had always been able to rely on her word.

She'd known Kyle for a matter of several weeks, discounting the two brief meetings at the hospital. Was that long enough to assess his character?

He'd sounded very convincing last night. And Tansy's sudden appearance had certainly reinforced his tale of unreasoning infatuation.

She saw a telephone box and drew up beside it. For several minutes she sat in the car, undecided. Then she climbed out and went to the telephone.

The line was engaged, and she retrieved her card with a mixture of disappointment and relief.

She laid her forehead for a few seconds against the cold hard wall of the booth. She'd give it one more try, then she could honestly say she'd made the attempt.

This time the ring went through, and Kyle answered almost instantly.

'Can you come here?' he asked her.

'I don't think that would be a good idea.' Tansy had said she was 'sort of tied up' for lunch. Supposing she went back to Kyle's apartment? Fler shuddered. She couldn't stand a repetition of last night.

'I'd like you to meet someone,' Kyle said. 'A friend of mine. If you won't come here, how about I see you at his place? I've just spoken to him, and he's free all day.'

'Who is he?'

'His name's Phil Morton.' Kyle paused as if silently debating something. 'He's a psychiatrist.'

\* \* \*

'My daughter's not crazy,' Fler told Phil Morton. A comfortable-looking man, dressed in bag-kneed trousers and a well-worn shirt, he'd been trimming some shrubs in his garden when she arrived. Kyle was already there, and now he sat with them at a slatted wooden table under the shade of a large umbrella, sipping on one of the cool drinks that Phil's wife had brought out before disappearing again into the rambling weatherboard house. Kyle had pushed his chair a little sideways, and was gazing towards the house, holding himself slightly aloof.

'From what Kyle's told me, I'd say you're probably right,' Phil said.

Fler cast Kyle a half-defensive, vindicated glance. He caught her eye but said nothing before resuming his contemplation of the house. Evidently he had decided not to take part in this discussion.

'But,' Phil added, making Fler sit up straighter, bracing herself, 'and also based on information from Kyle, I would guess she has developed an obsession with Kyle as the object.'

'Object?' Fler looked at Kyle again.

He gave a faint, rueful grin in her direction. 'I'm not flattered at the description.' Then he looked away again.

'The commonest factor in this kind of obsessive love,' Phil said in his slow, careful way, 'is a feeling of being rejected in childhood.'

'Tansy was never rejected.'

'I believe that you're divorced?'

'Yes, but Rick was a good father, even after the divorce. He didn't want custody, he couldn't have coped with a child—a teenager—and it would have cramped his lifestyle. But she used to stay with him often, he was good to her. Even spoiled her. He loved her.'

'Past tense?'

'Rick died two years ago——'

Kyle's head jerked round. 'Your husband *died*!'

'Ex-husband. Yes. When Tansy was in her last year at school. Quite suddenly.' She turned to Phil. 'It was hard for her, of course. She misses him, but she's coped well with the loss. She got very good marks in her last school exams.'

Phil sipped at his tall glass of juice. 'Hmm. You see, it isn't necessarily that anyone actually rejected her. When people die, most of us feel some quite irrational but well-documented emotions. Anger, for instance, is a very common component of grief.'

'You mean, even though he couldn't help it, deep down she feels he left her, deserted her?'

'Exactly. And then she met Kyle. Older, an authority figure. Perhaps a little like her father in some ways?'

Kyle stirred, put down his half-empty glass. He didn't appear to like being compared with Rick.

'Her father was a womaniser,' Fler said.

Kyle flashed her a smouldering look, his mouth tight.

Phil seemed to be hiding a smile. He glanced at Kyle, and said, 'Anyway, the girl was away from home, starting a new phase of her life, and at a vulnerable age. Her natural, normal need for security and affection has got a bit out of hand. That's all.'

Fler smiled at him with gratitude. He made it sound no big deal, something that could happen to anyone. Tansy had a problem, but it was a minor thing, it could be fixed.

'She probably needs treatment,' Phil said.

It was like a slap in the face. 'Treatment?' Drugs, hospitalisation?

'Therapy,' Phil said. 'But no one can force it on her. She has to realise herself that her behaviour is...inappropriate. She has to ask for help.'

'She won't.'

Kyle hitched his chair closer to the table. 'You're her mother,' he said. 'Can't you talk to her?'

'I tried,' Fler told him, 'this morning. She looked through me and insisted there was nothing wrong.'

He was looking at her penetratingly. '*You* know there's something wrong, don't you?' he asked her. 'Now?'

'I know she's...troubled,' Fler said. Pulling her gaze from his, she said to Phil, 'Is it possible to develop a full-blown obsession in the absence of any...reciprocation?'

'It's possible, certainly. You'll have heard of film stars being hounded by unknown fans. More commonly, there's been some kind of relationship to start with, but one party refuses to let go. Like the young man who shoots his ex-girlfriend rather than let someone else take his place. It's not so very rare. Still,' he added hastily, 'very few will go that far.'

Tansy wouldn't. Fler moistened her lips. 'She says Kyle made love to her. He denies it.'

Kyle made an abrupt movement, but didn't say anything. She had an impression that he was biting his tongue.

Phil glanced at him briefly, then looked back at Fler. 'I don't think I can comment on that,' he said. 'Except to say that for myself, as a friend, I would certainly be inclined to trust Kyle's word.'

'I've always been able to trust Tansy's.'

Phil nodded. 'It's your choice.'

'That's what Tansy said.'

Kyle said, 'I told you, Fler, Tansy's fantasising!' He appealed to Phil. 'Isn't that what these people do?'

*These people.* The phrase grated on Fler. She turned on him. 'You've admitted it isn't the first time a student's developed a crush on you. Surely if you were really uninterested from the beginning, you'd have been capable of making sure she got the message?'

He leaned across the table. 'Weren't you listening last night? Every time I thought I'd spelled out my complete uninterest in the clearest possible way she'd twist it around somehow in her own mind until it meant whatever she wanted it to! Sometimes I thought *I* was going mad!'

'Tansy's not mad!' Fler disclaimed hotly.

He sat back defeatedly.

Phil said mildly, 'It would be no disgrace if she was.'

'I know,' Fler said, ashamed of her reaction. 'But it would be ... worrying. You said you agreed with me that she isn't.'

He spread his hands. 'Without seeing her, I wouldn't know for sure. It's very unlikely. Not completely normal, though, on this one subject.'

'Would you see her, if I could persuade her?'

'If you like. Get in touch. Now, are you two going to join us for lunch? I have instructions from my wife to invite you.'

'Fler's having lunch with me,' Kyle said. 'Thanks all the same.'

She let him walk her to her car, parked out on the quiet street. 'Thank you,' she said. 'Phil was very helpful. I'll be getting on my way, now.'

'I'm taking you to lunch,' Kyle said. 'Remember?'

'I don't remember being invited. I thought it was a graceful way of making them not feel obliged to feed us both.'

He said, 'Actually, it was an ungraceful way of inviting you to eat with me. Alone. I want to talk to you, Fler. It was all I could think of.'

She wasn't sure if she wanted to be alone with him just yet. Ever. 'We talked last night.'

'And more.' He was studying her downbent head. 'I meant what I said last night, Fler. All of it.'

She raised her head then and looked at him. Last night he'd said he loved her. He'd told Tansy that he intended to make love to her mother.

'You told me last night that you believed me.'

Fler's distressed gaze flickered away from his, and he said, 'I'm not going to force a choice on you now. One thing I've learned over the past year: backing a person into a corner is no way to treat someone you profess to love. But last night... I wasn't making all the moves on my own. If you hadn't been reciprocating I'd have given it up long before we were so rudely interrupted. And I know you're not a woman who gives so much without her feelings being engaged.'

He stopped as if waiting for her to say something. But Fler didn't know what to say to him. Her feelings at the moment were numbed, battered.

Finally he said, an urgent undertone belying the determined calm of his voice, 'All I'm asking right now is lunch, in a public place. Is that too much?'

Fler shook her head. 'I just don't think I can take any more heavy discussion,' she said. 'Do you mind?'

He took her hand lightly in his. 'I don't mind. We'll talk about "shoes—and ships—and sealing wax"——'

'"Cabbages—and kings".' She looked up, smiling wanly.

'"And why the sea is boiling hot—and whether pigs have wings".' His answering smile glinted. 'Follow me again? Or shall we take my car?'

'I'll follow.'

This time he had chosen an outdoor venue, white tables and chairs in a garden setting, soft music playing in the background. They had salads and cold fruit drinks and talked, not of cabbages and kings but of recent books and old films and favourite beaches.

Kyle asked for a cheese board and ordered a half-carafe of fruity, crisp white wine. And at two-thirty Fler reluctantly looked at her watch and said, 'I have to go.'

He didn't argue, just paid the bill and went with her to her car. 'Glad you came?' he asked her quietly as he opened the door after she'd unlocked it.

'Yes.' She felt much more relaxed now, calmer. 'Thank you, Kyle.'

'You know I want to see you again.' As she raised her eyes he said almost roughly, 'Don't look like that. I told you I won't back you into any corners. Will you mind if I book myself into Manaaki next weekend?'

It was too soon. 'I need some time to think,' she said.

'I'll give you time,' he promised. 'Can I ask you one thing before you go? If Tansy wasn't...a factor, would you want to see me again?'

'Yes.' She owed him that much honesty. 'But——'

He put two warm fingers on her lips, closing them. 'That's all I need just now,' he told her. 'While you're doing your thinking, think about what you owe to yourself, will you? Not Tansy, not me. Yourself.'

He removed his fingers and replaced them with his mouth for a short, warming moment. 'I'll phone you,' he said. 'Tell me when.'

'I ... I'll phone *you*,' she said. And, at the quick, doubting frown in his eyes, 'I promise.'

## CHAPTER THIRTEEN

'I WANT to go down to Auckland to see Tansy again,' Fler told Rae two weeks later. 'Do you mind?'

'I know you're still worried about her. You go right ahead. The bookings are light now; it's no problem.'

Fler had written two letters, made three phone calls to Tansy. The letters drew no response, and the phone calls had been stilted on Tansy's side, determinedly 'normal' on Fler's. Last time she'd phoned, the girl who answered didn't know where Tansy was. 'She might be with Pat,' she added helpfully. 'He's out, too.'

This time she was invited into Tansy's room. The walls were hung with posters and the bed was rumpled and covered with clothes, her diary lying on the pillow. Tansy picked it up and put it on a shelf by the bed. She seemed reassuringly normal, a healthy glow on her skin, her hair soft and shiny. 'Lunch?' she repeated in answer to Fler's oh, so casual invitation. 'Yeah, fine. Where are you taking me?'

'You choose,' Fler suggested, watching as Tansy rapidly riffled through the jumble of clothes on the bed and chose a bright pink T-shirt to replace the blue one she was wearing over a pair of bottom-hugging jeans.

'There's a Mexican place we could try. They just opened.' Tansy peered into the mirror over the dressing-table, picked up a brush and flicked at her hair.

Standing behind her, Fler felt a little catch at her heart. Tansy was lovely, with the irreplaceable bloom of youth.

Her own face, reflected over her daughter's shoulder, looked like a blurred and faded copy. No man, surely, could prefer the older, worn and already subtly ageing version to that young, vital beauty.

Tansy turned. 'I'm ready.'

Fler smiled and put an arm about her shoulders. 'Good,' she said heartily. 'Let's go.'

Watching Tansy spoon into a confection of ice-cream, whipped cream, chocolate and fruit, Fler said, 'Do you remember I asked you if you'd thought about counselling, Tansy?'

Concentrating on the dessert, Tansy said coolly, 'I told you I don't need it.' Glancing up, she smiled. A blob of whipped cream on her upper lip made her look about six years old, Fler thought. 'Honestly,' she said. 'You don't need to worry about me.' Her eyes were clear and guileless.

'I just thought——'

'Anyway,' Tansy added, 'I'm too busy studying. And it would be expensive. A waste of time and money.'

It wasn't until she was about to get out of the car hours later that she turned to Fler and asked, 'Did you come down here to see Kyle?'

Startled, Fler said, 'No. No, I came to see you.'

'I'm all right now, you know.' Her eyes downcast, Tansy fiddled with a strand of hair hanging over her shoulder.

Fler reached over and brushed it back so she could see her daughter's face. 'Are you, darling?' Her eyes were anxious.

'I know he doesn't want me any more.' Tansy's voice trembled. She looked fully at her mother. 'Don't let him hurt you the way he hurt me!'

'Oh, Tansy!' Fler whispered. She pulled the girl into her arms, and soothed her hair while Tansy wept against her.

Finally Tansy pulled away, wiping her eyes with her hand. Fler handed her a tissue, and she blew her nose. 'Sorry,' she muttered.

'That's what mothers are for.' Fler stroked her hot cheek.

'I must look awful.'

'You're beautiful.'

Tansy grimaced. 'You're biased.'

'I know.' They smiled at each other, exchanging the familiar, teasing words. Fler said, 'Shall I come with you?'

Tansy shook her head. 'I'm all right. Thanks for lunch. See you.' She slid out of the car, and Fler watched her walk up the cracked path and let herself into the flat.

'Don't let him hurt you the way he hurt me.' The words reiterated themselves in her mind all the way home. She'd thought of phoning Kyle, of course she had. But after Tansy's warning, she couldn't bring herself to.

'Think about what you owe to yourself. Not Tansy, not me.' Kyle's voice. Warm, caring, concerned.

Was he really like that, or was it a façade that he used to make women fall for him? Phil had said he would trust him, as a friend. Friends could be biased. Rick's friends had covered for him, lied to Fler about where he was, who he was with, perhaps partly to spare her feelings, but also out of loyalty. There were rapists and murderers whose friends would testify in court to their good character.

Not that Kyle was in that class. But he had been ruthless with Tansy that night in his flat. Cold and hard.

He'd looked ready to do violence to her before Fler stopped him.

She shivered. Objectively, surely he was a man to stay away from. Wittingly or not, he was the reason Tansy had tried to kill herself, and he'd caused a rift in the always close relationship between Fler and her daughter.

And yet her body insisted on recalling with delight the way his lips and hands had touched her, her heart kept reacting to the echo of his voice in her mind, to the remembered light in his eyes as he looked at her.

'I won't see him again. I'll tell him I don't want to,' she resolved aloud. And was caught unaware by a sudden lump in her throat, an unbearable ache in her chest.

She wrote him a one-page letter, simply saying she thought it best if they didn't see each other any more, and wishing him well.

No reply came from Kyle. She told herself that he'd probably shrugged it off and gone on to conquer new fields. He was one of those men who couldn't help trying his luck with any reasonably good-looking woman. After her experience with Rick she ought to have known better. It was said that women tended to fall for men with the same faults, over and over. There were women who'd been married to two, even three, alcoholics in a row. And for some reason she was drawn to men who needed a processsion of women in their lives. She'd probably had a lucky escape.

Only try as she would she couldn't feel glad about it.

Tansy sent a couple of scrappy letters in answer to Fler's long, affectionate ones. Neither of them mentioned Kyle's name. Tansy seemed to be absorbed in her studies.

Then at Easter Fler came home from church on Good Friday afternoon to find Kyle's name written in his confident, cursive hand in the register.

'He arrived twenty minutes ago,' Rae told her. 'Asked if we had a spare room for the long weekend. Said he'd made a spur of the moment decision to get out of Auckland. I put him in Five. OK?'

'OK,' Fler echoed automatically; her heart was pounding erratically, the blood drumming in her forehead. Why had he come? What did he want? More than a weekend away from Auckland, surely. 'He was lucky,' she said. They'd had a cancellation the day before. Even though at Easter the weather tended to be unsettled and cool, Manaaki usually filled with optimists.

'Mmm. I told him,' Rae agreed. 'He said maybe it was fate.'

She didn't have to meet him alone the first time. The dining-room was full that evening, and she managed to give him an impersonal, friendly smile and hardly exchange two words with him. Afterwards he seemed happy talking to an elderly couple in the lounge, and Fler kept out of the way until everyone had gone to bed.

But the following day when she was picking up the newspaper the rural delivery van had left at the gate, she turned to find Kyle purposefully walking down the driveway towards her.

'Good morning.' She made to walk by him, but he stopped dead in front of her.

'When can I see you?' he asked bluntly. 'Alone.'

Fler's hands tightened on the rolled newspaper. 'I . . . hardly think that's necessary.'

There was a spark of anger in his eyes but his voice was even. 'I happen to think it is.'

When she didn't reply he went on, 'You did promise to phone me.'

'I wrote.'

'You can't just dismiss what happened between us in a few lines like that.'

'There isn't any more to say.'

'You could try giving me some reasons.'

'Do you need reasons?' Fler asked.

He looked at her in baffled silence. 'Yes,' he said. 'Yes, I think I do. You owe me that much.'

'You told me to think of what I owed myself.'

That seemed to check him for a second or two. Then he said, 'And did you?'

'Maybe I owe myself the right to say no.'

Slowly, he said, 'Maybe you do. But *I* owe it to myself to ask why.'

A couple of men carrying fishing rods came out of the front door of the house. Fler said, 'People are waiting for the paper. I have to go inside.'

'Give me an hour,' Kyle suggested. 'Whenever it suits you.'

The men came down the drive, bidding them good morning.

Kyle nodded to them, and Fler smiled, returning the greeting. She walked around Kyle and started up the drive.

'An hour,' he repeated, walking beside her. 'Surely you can spare me that much?'

They reached the steps. A cool morning breeze lifted from the sea and rustled the vines about the veranda. 'After lunch, then,' Fler said. 'I'll meet you on the beach.'

\*     \*     \*

He was waiting for her. The sky was washed with grey today, a wide sheet of metallic cloud overhead that thinned to pale blue out over the horizon, allowing flashes of intermittent sunshine. The sea was a choppy expanse of leaden grey-green broken by moving shards of white, the breeze fresh and cold. Kyle wore a windbreaker, his hands thrust into the pockets. Fler had put on a long natural wool sweater that came to mid-thigh over her jeans.

A couple of hardy fishermen were casting from the rocks at one end of the little beach. A family, warmly clothed against the chill, fossicked round the rock pools nearby, and a group of Maori women with buckets stood ankle-deep in the water, stooping to dig for *pipis* burrowing into the sand.

Fler and Kyle headed for the other end. The tide was out and they clambered over the wet, glistening rocks to enter the secluded little bay on the other side of the headland, with its cave and the fan of sand.

Kyle turned to help her jump from the rocks to the pebble-strewn sand. Automatically Fler took the hand he extended to her, feeling its strength as he steadied her. And its warmth.

He didn't let her go immediately, but when she looked up at him with a touch of hauteur he smiled slightly and released her fingers.

The tiny cove was more sheltered than the adjacent beach, and despite the waves riffling in further down the grey, stony apron it seemed quiet.

Kyle led the way to the uncluttered patch of soft sand and said, 'Shall we sit?'

He waited until Fler had settled herself with her legs stretched out before her and her back to a smooth rock wall before he dropped himself down not far from her, and raised one knee to rest a forearm across it while he surveyed her.

Fler removed her gaze from his, to stare at the horizon, a faint shimmer of silver sliced across the skyline.

'You told me last time we talked,' he said, 'that if Tansy weren't a factor you'd want to see me again. I have to assume that Tansy's the reason you decided against it, after all.'

Fler transferred her gaze to her fingers, linked loosely in her lap, while she tried to formulate an answer to that.

While she was still doing so, Kyle said, 'Tansy's nearly an adult. She's got a life of her own. She didn't even come home for Easter.'

She'd said she was going to spend Easter with friends in Tauranga. 'Did you expect her to be here?' Fler had wondered, she couldn't help it. In the light of his rejection of Tansy it seemed unlikely, but could he have changed his mind?

Kyle said, 'I hoped she wouldn't be. But I decided I'd take that chance, play it as it came. I needed to see you.'

Fler quelled a quick, rising gladness.

'How long,' Kyle asked, 'are you going to put Tansy's needs—or what you perceive are her needs—first? Aren't you entitled to a life, too?'

'I have a very nice life,' Fler said. 'You're jumping to conclusions, and they're wrong.'

'Tansy had nothing to do with your decision?' he challenged her.

'Not directly.' For the first time she looked at him. Her resolution wavered then. His gaze was sharp and steady, and there was some kind of pain there. She said, 'In the end I made the decision for my sake. Not anyone else's.'

He gave a curt little nod, as though accepting that. 'Can you explain that?'

'If you want it in words of one syllable, I don't need a man. Especially a man like——'

'A man like me,' he finished for her, grimly. 'So tell me what kind of man you think I am, Fler.'

She risked a glance at him. He looked both angry and controlled. Shrugging, she said, 'I don't know you that well.'

'Make up your mind,' he suggested. 'You apparently know enough to tell me you don't want anything more to do with me. I've been judged and condemned, and I haven't even been told what the charges are!'

'I'm not condemning you.'

'No? It feels remarkably like it to me. Do you know what I think?' Without waiting for her to reply, he went on, 'I think that husband of yours hurt you so much that you're afraid to put your trust in any man. Isn't that it?'

'Have you been talking to your friend Phil lately?'

The ghost of a grin flickered across his mouth. 'No. I worked it out all by myself.'

Possibly he had a point, too. 'I just don't feel ready for another relationship.'

'How many have you had?'

Her eyes lifted to his face. 'If it's any of your business, I haven't had any. Not since Rick.'

'And your divorce was...how long ago?'

'Five years. Contrary to popular opinion, a divorced woman isn't necessarily panting for sex with every stray male who crosses her path. I suppose you thought I'd be easily persuaded into bed. Sorry to disappoint you.'

'I thought nothing of the kind!' he snapped. 'And no matter what popular opinion is, I certainly never thought you were "panting for sex". I resent the implication that you're making. I'm beginning to see what you meant by that remark about "my sort of man". And I damn well resent that, too! Let me tell you, I am *not* like your husband!'

'You never knew him.'

'You told me—told Phil—he was a womaniser.'

Fler looked at him. 'Well?'

He took a deep, angry breath. 'Well, *I'm not!*' He glared at her in frustration. 'Is this Tansy's doing?'

'All she said was she hoped I wouldn't be hurt as she had been.'

Kyle stood up, walked a few paces and then swung round. 'It always comes back to Tansy, doesn't it?' he said bitterly. 'Can't you see, Fler? The girl is *sick!*'

'But you did hurt her!' Fler cried. '*You did!*'

He came back and knelt at her side, grasping her shoulders. 'So she was hurt,' he said. 'I'm sorry about that. But I can't help it.'

That was what Rick had used to say. '*I didn't mean to hurt you, honey. I just couldn't help it.*'

'Fler,' Kyle urged. 'I know she's your daughter, but try to stand back a bit. I told you I love you. I know you feel something for me, you've tacitly admitted it, although you won't allow yourself the words. Are you going to allow a hysterical teenager to wreck that for us?'

'She wasn't hysterical,' Fler argued. She'd been quite calm then. Rational. And sincere. Fler would have staked her life on it.

'Whatever,' Kyle said. 'You must admit her reaction to seeing us together at my flat was...extreme. She'd do anything to keep us apart.'

'I know my daughter,' Fler insisted stubbornly. 'It wasn't like that at all.'

Kyle dropped his hands and shrugged. 'As you say. So where does that leave us?'

Nowhere, Fler supposed, with a wrenching feeling of grief. It would have been easier if he had accepted her dismissal. She had been coping quite well with the numbing depression that had enveloped her over the past several weeks. But now, with his physical presence so near, the prospect of losing him again was an actual pain somewhere near her heart.

The wind found its way into the cove and momentarily lifted the hair back from his forehead, sharpening the outlines of his profile as he stared at the water, frowning. It carried the scent of him, soap and musk and a hint of salty sea, to Fler, and she stirred restlessly, wanting to touch him, smooth his windblown hair, put her lips to the grim line of his mouth and soften it.

He turned to her then, and must have seen something in her face. An answering emotion flared in his eyes, and he made a quickly checked movement towards her. He rocked back on his heels, staring into her eyes with a compelling, almost pleading gaze, and repeated, 'Where, Fler?'

'I . . . don't know. Where do you want us to be, Kyle?'

Wry humour lifted a corner of his mouth. 'If I told you that, all your darkest suspicions would be confirmed.' Then he said, 'I want to make love to you. You know that. But I want more. I promised not to crowd you, not to push. But surely the fact that I'm here, that I didn't just toss your letter away and go out and find someone to console me, must tell you something?'

'It wouldn't have been too hard,' she said, 'finding someone to do that?'

Warily he said, 'I don't keep a little black book, if that's what you mean. Nor anything like it. I was speaking metaphorically. Or is it rhetorically?'

'You're the professor.'

'Not yet, actually.'

'Some day, I suppose.'

'Maybe.'

She looked at him thoughtfully. 'So why me? I have no degree. I'm not an intellectual.'

'Haven't you got the message yet?' He leered. 'I love you for your body.'

Fler laughed on a little catch in her throat.

'That's better,' Kyle said, and took her hand in his. 'You don't have to have a degree to be intelligent, witty, interesting.'

Fler shook her head. 'Interesting?' She hadn't pulled her hand away. It felt right, cradled into his. Did he love her? Or was it his way of saying that he wanted to make love to her? Even Rick had made a distinction between the two. *'I love you, honey. With the others it's just sex, it doesn't mean anything.'*

'Interesting,' Kyle confirmed. 'I find you fascinating.'

Fler blinked. She couldn't believe this. 'Why?'

'Your strength, I think,' he said musingly. 'Courage. Independence. Compassion. Some kind of certainty about life that's rare. A capacity for loving that I want for myself. Directed to myself. Your interest in new things, new knowledge, experiences. Although you're cautious about that last, aren't you?' He slanted a smile at her. 'And the occasional glimpse of insecurity, like the way you seem unable to believe that I find you madly attractive.'

Fler gave a little negative movement of her head.

'Why not?' Kyle demanded. 'Quite apart from all that, you have a lovely face, and very desirable body. Not that I can see much of it under that.' He ran his eyes over the thick jersey.

'It's a thirty-seven-year-old face,' she reminded him, 'and body. Nearly thirty-eight. Every day of your working life you stand facing a crowd of *teenagers*, for heaven's sake. Gorgeous young girls.'

'Not all of them are that,' he pointed out. 'Quite a number are mature students. And not all the young ones are gorgeous. Some, I'll admit, are pleasant to look at. When I was eighteen myself I'd have found one or two of them irresistible. I'm not eighteen any more. I want something more in a woman. Some...maturity.'

'Experience?'

'Are you putting words in my mouth? If you mean sexual experience, that isn't what I was talking about.'

Fler drew her knees up and clasped her hands around them, studying her thumbnails. He was being persuasive again. She could feel the pull of his personality, drawing her closer, not physically but emotionally.

She glanced at him and away again. He wanted her. He'd said so. Who was she trying to fool? Half the attraction was physical. Perhaps more than half. Just knowing that he found her desirable was a powerful aphrodisiac.

'Fler?' His hand brushed her cheek. His fingers curved about her chin, making her face him.

Her palms were damp. There was a faint fluttering in her stomach.

'Fler?' he said, his voice deep and quiet, almost drowned by the hushed hurrying of the sea. 'Fler, I desperately want to kiss you.'

Her lips parted, and she saw his head lower and blot out the light. Then his mouth was on hers, his hands slipping about her to bring her closer, her head tipping back against his encircling arm.

His mouth moved over hers almost feverishly, tasting, caressing, claiming. She ought to be saying no. But not yet. This was too new, too exciting. Deliberately she blotted out thoughts, doubts. Just for a few minutes, she promised herself. There was no harm in a kiss. She let him coax her lips further apart, deepening the kiss, starting a slow, spiralling heat throughout her body.

His hand burrowed under the bulky jersey and the T-shirt beneath that, and his fingers found the line of her spine, the warm flesh over her ribs, the soft mound under the bra, with its hardening centre.

Easing her down on the sand, he lifted his mouth and smiled at her, his eyes brilliant, admiring. 'We got to this stage once before,' he said. 'I hope this time we'll be undisturbed.' His hands were both inside her shirt, now. She bit her lip as they closed on her breasts, sure and intimate.

Kyle said, 'Am I hurting you?' The delicious stroking paused.

Fler shook her head. 'Don't stop.' She hadn't meant to say that, she ought to stop him, her mind said, but it was overridden by her clamouring senses.

'I certainly don't want to.' He watched her face, enjoying the play of expression over it as he resumed his gentle caresses of her body. Her eyelids fluttered down, half-closed, her breath coming quickly through parted lips. She touched a finger to the hollow in his throat where his shirt was open, let her hand fall until it encountered the tautness of his jeans over his thighs, and ran her palm over it, smiling as the glitter in his eyes intensified.

Kyle's hands slid down and shaped her waist, a thumb gently pressing on the hollow of her navel. She felt the snap fastening of her jeans part, the long jersey still hiding what he was doing, even when he rasped the zip down.

It had been a long time since a man had touched her this way. She closed her eyes, her head moving to one side. Then his breath was on her cheek, his teeth teasing her ear, until he breathed, 'Kiss me, Fler.' And she turned blindly and found his mouth, clinging, opening, thrusting, while he lay beside her with one leg between hers, and his fingers caressed her.

She raised her arms and hung them round his neck, ran her fingers into his hair, and inside the collar of his shirt, along his hard shoulders. The rhythmic pounding of the waves echoed the pounding of her blood; she couldn't distinguish between them. She felt the build-up of sensation and tore her mouth from his and gasped, 'Stop! It's...'

His face was taut and flushed, but he smiled down at her frantic eyes. 'Why? You like it, don't you? It feels as though you like it.'

'Too much! But you——?'

He bent to press a brief, hot kiss on her mouth. 'I like it, too. I want to do this for you, Fler. I want to see your face when I pleasure you. Let me. Trust me.' He kissed her cheek, her throat, and returned again to her mouth.

When she stiffened, poised on the edge, he felt it and lifted his head, smiling down, his sea-coloured eyes avid for her reaction. Then waves of sensation took her, and she shuddered against his firm, knowing hand, her eyes closing while long, gasping moans of pleasure parted her lips and her head tossed from side to side on the sand.

For a long time afterwards she lay still, her eyes closed. He stroked her gently for a little longer, and then did up the zip he had undone, and the fastener. He gathered her closer against him, and kissed her cheek again, murmuring, 'You were beautiful, darling. Thank you.'

He was thanking *her*? Filled with a grateful well-being and a sensuous lethargy, she thought it ought to be the other way about. She said, leaning her head against his shoulder, 'Don't you want . . . ?'

Faint laughter shook him. 'Oh, yes. I want. Very much so. There's a rather convenient cave right behind us that I'm sorely tempted to drag you into—by the hair if necessary. But I've just noticed that the tide has been creeping up on us while we were . . . otherwise engaged. I think our time may be up.'

'We can't have been here that long!' Fler turned and stared at the encroaching sea.

They had. She scrambled up, pushing sand-dusted hair from her eyes. 'Oh, heavens! Rae will be expecting me back. We have to go!'

# CHAPTER FOURTEEN

THEY got wet to the waist scrambling on to the rocks and then off again at the other side against the rising tide.

Before they started up the path to Manaaki, Kyle grasped her arm, and said in a low voice, 'May I come down to visit you tonight?'

Heat rising to her wind-cooled face, Fler nodded. She couldn't deny him, now. They'd gone too far to turn back.

Dripping, Fler apologised to Rae for being late, ignoring her speculative glance at Kyle who was right behind her. 'I'll get changed and be with you in a tick,' she promised.

She showered, trying to banish the erotic images that still held her body in thrall, shampooed her hair quickly under the running water, and changed into a fresh blouse and skirt. A few quick passes of the blow-dryer over her hair followed by a ruthless combing made her more presentable, but there was nothing she could do about the peculiarly languid look of her eyes, or the faint flush that still coloured her cheeks.

Tactfully, Rae held her tongue and didn't even comment when she had to repeat a question two or three times before Fler responded. But as she was shrugging into a jacket before leaving that night, she gave Fler a penetrating look and said, 'Take care.'

The look momentarily shook Fler out of her dream world. 'Yes,' she said. Rae was worried. She'd seen Fler and Kyle come in from the beach, and she was a very astute woman. Fler had told her that Kyle was the reason Tansy had overdosed on pills.

Tansy. All day Fler had almost succeeded in relegating Tansy to the back of her mind. But later that night when she closed the door of her own quarters behind her, she wasn't able to do so any longer. There was the photograph of herself and Tansy standing on the bookcase under the window, the tapestry picture that at twelve years old Tansy had painstakingly stitched for her mother hung on the wall. And on her way to the bathroom Fler passed the open door of her daughter's room.

Drawn by a reluctant compulsion, she went in, absently noting its unnatural neatness. She sat on the striped bedcover, an ancient doll and a one-eared rabbit staring at her glassy-eyed from the pillow. A poster of blue-eyed Siamese kittens was pinned to the wall over the bed, and on the dressing-table a mirror, brush and comb were watched over by a large musical doll in a faded blue lace crinoline. Tansy had won it in a raffle when she was nine. On the bedside table was a precisely aligned row of music cassettes and a picture of her father.

Fler picked up the photograph, studied the handsome, laughing face. Sadness gripped her. For Rick, who'd been too young to die at forty-one, cut down prematurely and with numbing suddenness by a virulent form of meningitis. For Tansy, who'd lost him at sixteen. For herself, and her broken dreams. The Rick she thought she'd married had been lost to her long before.

Was Kyle another one like him? The thought surfaced, unbidden.

Her heart said no. But her head reminded her of her earlier gullibility. It had been years before she'd let herself believe the blatant evidence of Rick's infidelity. Before she'd been no longer able to accept the excuses, the lies.

'Trust me,' Kyle had said.

She wanted to. Abruptly, she put down the photograph and stood up. And heard the discreet knocking on the outer door.

She halted, for a second tempted to pretend she wasn't here. Silly, of course. Kyle knew she was here. She'd invited him. And he expected, tonight, to share her bed.

The tapping came again, slightly louder. She drew a quick breath, and went to let him in.

She was relieved to see that he was dressed in a white open-necked shirt and casual dark trousers. Hastily she banished from her mind an absurd expectation of Kyle arriving on her doorstep in pyjamas and a robe. Of course he wouldn't wander through the house like that. It was still quite early; anyone might be about.

And that thought, with its furtive undertones, made her feel immediately that this meeting was somehow sordid.

'Come in,' she said automatically, and stepped back.

He was carrying a green bottle with a gold-foil top. 'I know it's a cliché,' he said, as he saw her eyeing it. 'But note that I didn't bring you flowers.'

His eyes invited her to share the joke. Trying to dispel the sudden depression that had settled on her, she forced a smile to her lips. 'Why not?'

'Red roses are out of season,' he said promptly. 'And nothing else would do.' His eyes questioned her, then he glanced around, found a small table to put the bottle down on, and said, 'Come here.'

She went into his arms, willing herself to respond to the touch of his lips on hers, to let her body meld itself against the firm male contours of his.

But she knew she was stiff and unsure, and in a little while he raised his head and stared down at her, enquiring softly, 'What's wrong?'

What *was* wrong with her? Fler asked herself. This afternoon she had melted in his arms, all her defences down. She'd agreed that he could come here tonight, implied that she was willing to carry on where they'd left off. It was both stupid and unfair to keep blowing hot and cold like this. He'd get sick of it and——

And leave her.

'I've had a long day,' she said. She eased herself out of his arms. 'Shall I chill this?' She picked up the bottle of wine, holding it with both hands in front of her.

'Good idea,' Kyle said after subjecting her to a narrow-eyed stare. 'I suppose you have some suitable glasses.'

'Somewhere in the back of the cupboard. I could fetch some from the dining-room if I can't find them.'

He followed her, lounging in the doorway of the kitchen while she placed the bottle in the freezer. She opened a cupboard, stood on tiptoe, craning. 'In here, I think.'

Kyle strolled forward, took her shoulders to move her aside. 'I'll get them.'

He reached, turning with two flutes in his hands to find she'd moved away and was by the sink.

'They'll need rinsing,' she said. 'I haven't used them for ages.'

She made a business of doing it, polishing them afterwards with a teatowel while Kyle watched in silence, finding a tray to put them on. All the time she hardly looked at him, and the tension in the kitchen grew.

She fiddled with the glasses, aligning them carefully dead centre, side by side. The telephone shrilled from her bedroom, and she said, 'Excuse me,' and hurried to answer it.

Afterwards she had to go through to the office to consult the reservations book, and when she came back Kyle was standing in the lounge waiting for her.

'The bubbly will need another few minutes chilling,' he said. 'You look bothered, Fler. Why don't we sit down for a while and just talk?'

'Talk?'

He smiled, stepping forward to take her hand and draw her down beside him on the sofa. 'We've done it before,' he said. 'You're as nervy as a cat. Are you afraid I'm about to leap on you and have my wicked way with you?'

'You're not that crude.' Not crude at all. Perhaps he was exceedingly clever.

'I should hope not,' he said. He looked down at her fingers, linked in his, and then spread them across his palm. 'You have lovely hands.'

'Nonsense.' Her hands were capable, working hands with short, unvarnished nails. Occasionally she remembered to rub some cream into them, but more often not.

'They are,' Kyle insisted. 'When you touched me this afternoon, it felt good. Strong. Very sexy.'

She hadn't touched him as intimately as he had her. But she felt herself flushing and snatched her hand away.

Kyle laughed. 'You're shy?'

Stiffly, Fler said, 'I suppose that's silly, at my age.'

'Surprising,' Kyle corrected. 'Not silly.' He leaned back into the corner of the sofa, looking at her. 'I wish you'd tell me what's worrying you.'

'Nothing.' Fler looked away.

He stood up. 'I'll go and check on the wine.'

When he came back he was carrying the tray, bearing two glasses and the opened bottle with a curl of vapour escaping from it.

'Maybe this will help you relax,' he suggested, handing her a glass when he had filled them. 'Have some Madeira, my dear!' he added sinisterly, raising his own glass.

Fler managed a short, breathy, little laugh. It wasn't Madeira, it was a light, fruity, champagne-style wine with a pleasant tang. 'It's delicious,' she said sincerely.

'Good. I chose it carefully.' As if reading her mind, he said, 'I didn't bring it with me from Auckland. I went scouting before dinner.'

Fler made a conscious effort to relax, sinking back against the sofa cushions, sipping her wine.

The glass was empty quite soon, and when Kyle enquired, 'Another?' she mutely held it out for him.

She tensed as he moved closer to pour it, but when he'd finished he leaned back again, regarding her with a thoughtful expression. 'When you said you'd had a long day,' he said finally, 'was that a hint? A variation on, "I have a headache tonight, dear"?'

'No,' Fler denied. 'I didn't mean it like that. But——'

'Ah!' Kyle was inspecting his wine, gazing down into the tulip-shaped glass. 'I had a feeling there was a *but* somewhere in the offing.'

Rattled at the dryness of his tone, she said, 'I'm sorry. I'm just a bit... unused to this kind of... relationship.' She took a gulp of her wine. She couldn't go back now on her implied word. 'It's all right,' she said, 'really.'

'Is it?' He downed his drink and put the glass on the table near by.

On the beach Kyle had concentrated solely, unselfishly on giving her pleasure. Surely he had a right to expect her to do the same for him, tonight? Or at least her willingness to make the pleasure mutual. And maybe, an insidious voice whispered, that was just what he'd counted on. That she'd feel obliged to follow through. She licked her lower lip, tasting the wine. His wine. She sipped at it again, met his eyes and said, 'Of course.'

His answering gaze was puzzled and angry, maybe a little wary. After a moment he leaned across and took the still half-full glass from her hand to place it beside his. He gripped her shoulders and pulled her towards him, his eyes searching hers, a hard, enquiring light in them, before he brought his mouth down and kissed her with desperate passion.

*Yes*! something inside her said fiercely. *Yes*. Close off the doubts, the fears, never mind tomorrow. Tonight I'll have this. Tonight he's mine. And I'm his.

She kissed him back unreservedly, almost feverishly, trying to blank out all thought, everything but the hot, wanton feelings he was arousing with his mouth, his hands that were finding her shoulders, breasts, thighs, his body as he bore her backwards until she half lay against the cushions.

With his hand resting on her hip, he raised his head and said, 'Before this goes any further, Fler, are you going to invite me into your bed?'

She swallowed. From the corner of her eye she could see the bookcase, the photograph of herself and Tansy. Trying not to think about it, she said, 'That's what you want, isn't it?'

A faint frown brought his brows together. 'Isn't it what you want, too?'

She swallowed. Admitted, 'Yes.'

'Well, then,' he said softly, the frown clearing, 'what are we waiting for?'

He got up and drew her to her feet beside him. She managed to avoid looking at the photograph, but as he urged her into the short passageway, an arm about her waist, his lips nuzzling at her hair, her temple, he stopped at the doorway of Tansy's room, not knowing which was Fler's bedroom.

'No,' she said, turning towards her own room. 'In here.'

He turned with her, and closed the door one-handed behind them, led her to the bed and sat on the edge for a little while, just kissing and touching, before they lay side by side, body to body. The bedside lamp was on, and he didn't suggest they turn it off. She was glad he hadn't undressed yet, hadn't wanted her naked as soon as they entered the room. She'd gone cold, her mood abruptly flattened as they hesitated at Tansy's door. Perhaps he'd sensed it, was willing to take the time to coax her back to receptiveness.

It didn't happen. She made some feeble attempt at pretence, but in the end he drew away from her. 'This isn't working for you,' he said roughly. 'Is it?' And sat up with his back to her, on the edge of the bed, doing up the buttons of his shirt and running a hand over his hair.

'I'm sorry,' Fler whispered. 'I thought... I know you had a right to...'

'A right?' His head turned swiftly. 'What right?'

'I mean, I owed you... something. After what you did for me... earlier.'

He stared at her as though he'd never seen her before. Then he stood up, took two swift strides away from the bed, and swung to face her again. 'Let me get this straight,' he said, sounding as though his teeth were gritted. 'You said I could come to your room, brought me in here to your bed, kissed me, let me try to make love to you, because you thought you *owed it to me*?'

Fler sat up, raking her own hair back behind her ears with her fingers, conscious that her clothes were dishevelled, her skirt riding above her knees. She pulled it down. 'It wasn't exactly like that,' she hedged. 'But I thought...that you hoped for some sort of...reciprocation.'

He clamped his teeth together as though biting back some explosive remark. His face, even in the dim light, seemed suddenly paler. 'What I hoped was that you felt something like what I feel for you. The last thing I wanted was to put you under some kind of sexual duress. If that's the sort of bastard you think I am,' he said, 'heaven help us both.'

'I don't *know* what you are!' Fler said, despairingly. 'That's the problem, Kyle! I don't really know you—do I?'

'No,' he said, 'that's not the problem. The problem is you don't trust me. You want some kind of proof that I'm not what Tansy told you I am. That I'm not like your ex-husband. I can't give you proof, Fler. All I can give you is myself, and my word. And it's not enough. Is it?'

'When I'm with you,' she tried to explain, 'I believe you.'

'And when you're with Tansy you believe her,' he reminded her ruthlessly. 'You think I seduced her and then dumped her, and lied about it to you in order to seduce you as well.'

'No!'

'What else?' he enquired bitterly. 'You just said—implied—that's what you believe when I'm not here on the spot arguing differently. You may not believe it right now this minute, but tomorrow, or next week, we'll be right back to square one again. I love you, I want you. I want some kind of future with you. But it isn't going to work, is it? We can't live like that. We can't ... be with each other on that basis.'

'I want you, too,' Fler said, not quite ready to say she loved him, but feeling her heart tear at the thought of losing him.

For a second his eyes lit, but then the quick flame died. 'Yes,' he said tiredly. He turned away, walking towards the door. 'But it isn't enough.' He wrenched at the handle and paused in the doorway, looking back at her. 'I'm sorry, Fler. I promised I wouldn't back you into a corner, and it seems that's what I've done. I shouldn't have come here.'

He left the door open, but seconds later she heard the door into the public part of the house close with a decisive snap.

She sat huddled on the bed for a long time, feeling stunned and empty.

While she was at church the following morning, Kyle checked out.

'Changed his mind, he said,' Rae told her. 'He insisted on paying for the two extra days, but said he'd got to go back unexpectedly to Auckland. Did you two have a fight?'

'What makes you think that?'

Rae gave her a look. 'All right,' she said cheerfully, 'but I wasn't born yesterday.' With a more searching glance, she added, 'If you want to talk ... ?'

'Thanks, Rae. Maybe some time.' Rae was a good listener, but Fler didn't think that talking was going to change anything.

'Oh, I forgot,' Rae added. 'He's lost a cufflink. Said if we find it would we be sure and post it registered. It's one of a pair his parents gave him on his twenty-first birthday, gold with a small garnet set into it. I'll tell the maids to watch for it.'

'Yes,' Fler said. 'Do that.' Had he been wearing his cufflinks last night? She didn't remember. After putting away her bag and changing her church-going shoes for more comfortable ones, she searched the bedroom and lounge but found no gold cufflink. Perhaps it would turn up in his room.

One of the maids slipped on the stairs and sprained her ankle. For the rest of the long weekend Fler was kept busy with the guests. If it didn't exactly keep her mind off Kyle it effectively stopped her from taking any action.

Although, what action could she take? Kyle had simply walked out; he didn't see any future for them. He'd given up.

Then, when most of the guests had departed, Tansy unexpectedly came home.

'I got the chance of a lift,' she informed Fler as she dumped a backpack on the lounge floor. 'Saves me a bus fare and I thought, Why not?'

'Aren't you supposed to be back at university this week?'

Tansy grimaced. 'It's a short week. Anyway, the girl who brought me is going back tomorrow, so I'm only staying one night. Aren't you pleased to see me?'

'Of course I'm pleased.' Fler gave her a hug. But there was an edginess about Tansy that rang warning bells in Fler's mind. 'How was Tauranga?'

A shrug. 'OK, I guess. I might be moving out of the flat.'

'Oh? I thought you liked it there.' Fler sat on the arm of one of the chairs, prepared to listen.

Tansy flung herself on to the sofa. 'I had a row with Pat. In Tauranga. His parents' place.'

'Is that where you went? His parents?'

'It doesn't *mean* anything!' Tansy said scornfully. 'We're just friends. Flatmates. I've never been to Tauranga before. I thought it would be fun.'

Fler said carefully, 'He seems quite fond of you.'

'He thinks he's the big brother I never had. I told him I never wanted one.' Tansy looked up, her eyes sparkling with temper.

'Perhaps he's a bit overprotective,' Fler suggested. 'What happened?'

'Nothing happened.' Tansy sighed impatiently. 'I told him about Kyle. We were talking,' she said, 'and...somehow I wanted to.' She rolled her eyes heavenward. '*That* was a mistake.'

'What exactly did you tell him?' Fler asked, keeping her voice steady.

'Everything. He didn't say a word until I'd finished, and then he just flipped. He said...' Tansy stopped, scowling. 'All sorts of things.'

'Like what?'

'That I was acting like a moronic adolescent, for one,' Tansy said darkly. 'And that was one of the more complimentary things he called me! I tell you, he's nuts!'

'You don't think...' *that there might be some truth in what Pat said?* But Tansy's hostile yet vulnerable stare stopped her in mid-sentence. Cravenly, she said, 'How about putting away your bag, and I'll make you a special dinner, just for us. They can do without me in the dining-room tonight.'

Neither Pat nor Kyle was mentioned again that night. Over breakfast Fler said, 'Don't be too hasty about moving out of the flat, will you? I expect Pat is sorry for some of the things he said. I'm sure he didn't mean to hurt you.'

Tansy blinked away a tear. 'I wasn't hurt, I was furious.'

'And hurt,' Fler insisted. 'You're quite fond of him, too, aren't you? In a sisterly way,' she added hastily.

'I suppose.' Tansy sawed savagely at a piece of toast. 'I just think he ought to mind his own business.' She finished up the toast, emptied her coffee-cup and said, 'Do you want me to put my sheets in the wash?'

'Mmm, please. I'll be washing today, so you may as well.' Fler stood up, stacking the plates. 'Would you mind stripping my bed for me, too, while I get these dishes done?' Tansy had always hated doing dishes; they had a tacit arrangement that she'd do any chores but that.

Fler had stacked the dishes on the draining board and was letting water out of the sink when Tansy came into the kitchen, a strange, set look on her face, holding something in her hand.

'Darling?' Fler said. 'What is it?'

'This.' Tansy opened her hand.

Fler looked at the gold cufflink on her palm. 'Where did you find it?' she asked blankly.

The girl's pale lips barely moved. 'In your bed.'

Fler shook her head. 'But I looked——' She swallowed and met Tansy's shocked, accusing eyes. 'Tansy——'

'It was wedged into the corner of the frame, almost under the mattress,' Tansy said. 'I wouldn't have noticed, except that I shoved the mattress over too far when I was putting on the clean sheet. It's Kyle's, isn't it?'

It had his initials on it, and in any case, she had never lied to Tansy. 'Yes,' Fler said. 'It's Kyle's. But——'

'You've been having an affair with him.'

'That's not true——'

'I suppose you've been l-laughing at me behind my back!' Her blue eyes went wide and tragic, filled with tears.

'Of course we haven't!' Fler said. 'We wouldn't! Tansy, listen to me!'

'*No*!' Tansy backed from her, shaking her head. Ignoring Fler's protests, she went on, her voice rising, overriding her mother's. 'Kyle said he wasn't interested in me because I'm too young. But *you're* not, are you? You're certainly old enough! You convinced me before, but it was all *lies*! How long have you been sleeping with him?'

'*I am not sleeping with him*!' Fler found herself shouting. 'Stop it, Tansy!'

Tansy's face was flushed and streaked with tears. Her fist was clenched once more on the cufflink she held. Suddenly she drew back her hand and threw it, aiming for Fler's face. Fler blinked and jerked her head aside, felt the small impact on her temple before the cufflink fell to the floor with a muffled tinkle.

Instantly it was followed by a much louder sound as Tansy's arm swept the freshly washed dishes from the bench to shatter at her feet.

'Tansy!'

She took no notice. A vase from the table followed, and like a dervish the girl darted from one part of the kitchen to another, picking up plates, snatching cups, smashing everything in sight in an orgy of destruction. Within seconds the floor was littered with shards of china and glass. Sobbing, panting, between horrendous crashes she cried, 'You took him away from me... just like you sent Daddy away! You just... don't want me to have anyone of my own!' She picked up a lone glass that had escaped the carnage, still sitting innocently on a corner of the counter.

Fler held her breath, her heart beginning a sudden hard pounding as an expression almost of cunning flitted across Tansy's face. She watched in horror as the glass was lifted and smashed against the edge of the bench, leaving a jagged half in Tansy's hand.

Tansy's head was bent, but even before she lifted the wrist of the other hand, the vulnerable inner side uppermost, Fler was frantically hurling herself across the room, screaming, '*Tansy*!'

Tansy's head jerked up, her eyes strangely blind, and the hand holding the glass came up, too, wielding it like a weapon in front of her.

But it wasn't the gleaming, deadly points of glass that stopped Fler short, inches away from the vicious threat. That sent her suddenly icy cold with appalled disbelief. It was the hatred in her daughter's eyes.

'Tansy!' It was a whisper this time.

Her eyes locked on the girl's face, she saw the hatred turn to horror, to a disbelief that equalled her own. To a blank bewilderment.

Slowly the glass lowered, and Tansy fumblingly replaced it on the bench. Her gaze still on her mother, she said in the tearful, whimpering, breathless voice of a frightened child, 'Mummy—*I need help*.'

## CHAPTER FIFTEEN

FLER parked her car, took a deep breath and got out. She knew Kyle was home. Her brief telephone call had confirmed that, although he hadn't sounded particularly keen to see her. His voice had been cool and formal.

Then, perhaps, so had hers.

After she rang the bell there was a pause. She was wondering if she ought to press the button again when Kyle opened the door.

He was casually dressed in trousers and a shirt with the collar open, the sleeves rolled. But she hardly noticed, her gaze flying immediately to his face.

Which told her nothing. It was as if he'd deliberately wiped all expression from it before coming to the door. He passed a lightning glance over her carefully chosen fine grey wool skirt and jacket and soft heather-coloured blouse, then stepped back. 'Come in.'

The room seemed warm, and before taking the seat he silently waved her to she slipped off her jacket, folding it over the arm of the chair.

Kyle was still standing. 'Can I get you a drink?'

'No, thank you.' How stilted they sounded. Like strangers. She slipped down the strap of her shoulder bag and opened the clasp. 'I brought you this,' she said, holding out a white envelope.

He stepped forward and took it from her, tipped out the cufflink into the palm of his hand. 'Where was it?'

'In...in my bed.' She moistened her lips. 'Tansy found it.'

178

She saw his hand close hard on the gold square, so hard it must have hurt. '*Oh, God*!' He swung away from her. 'Precipitating another crisis, I suppose.' Across the room now, he turned again to face her.

'It did, rather.' She remembered her kitchen littered inches deep with broken crockery, smashed glass, Tansy threatening her with a broken glass. 'I really thought she'd got over her... infatuation with you.'

He shoved the cufflink into his pocket. 'So did I. She'd stopped phoning. I got a card on Valentine's Day,' he said wryly. 'Obviously expensive, but unsigned. Could have been anyone. Once I thought I saw her hanging about near here, but I decided I was just being paranoid.'

Fler shook her head. 'She knew you'd seen her.'

*I know it was pathetic,* Tansy had said in self-disgust. *He didn't want me, only I couldn't seem to help myself. I'd just hang about outside his place, watching.*

'She's having therapy,' Fler said. 'She let me phone Phil.'

Kyle sat down abruptly on the arm of the sofa. 'It's about time. How did you talk her into it?'

'I didn't. As Phil told us, she had to make the decision herself.' Some day she might tell Kyle the full story. If there was to be a some day for them. She said, 'I could have posted the cufflink, but Rae said you valued it. I thought it would be safer to deliver it myself.'

'Did you?'

He wasn't going to meet her halfway, that was obvious. He'd closed off his emotions from her. Or perhaps his feelings for her had died. If so, they had never really run that deep.

No, she said to herself. Don't do this to him again. She'd always discounted Kyle's declared feelings for her, afraid to believe in him, to trust him. But he wasn't shallow, or fickle, or an opportunist. He was honest and principled and he'd said that he loved her.

She said, 'Tansy thought that we were lovers.'

'I'm sure you enlightened her about that.' He sounded cynical, almost bored.

'I told her that we had never been lovers,' Fler said. 'But that I love you.'

In the silence she could hear the traffic outside, a distant siren, the rustle of wind in unseen leaves.

Kyle might have been carved in stone. Then he stood up quite slowly. 'Say that again.'

'I said...' her voice trembled '...that I love you.'

She saw him swallow. 'Why,' he asked carefully, 'are you telling me this now?'

She had to fight down a hysterical giggle. It wasn't exactly the reaction she'd expected. 'Because,' she said helplessly, 'I thought...it might...might matter to you.'

'Oh, it *matters*!' he said almost violently. He made a movement towards her and then checked himself visibly. As though the words were wrenched unwillingly from him, he said, 'What about Tansy?'

Fler's eyes pleaded with him. 'Try to understand, Kyle. We have to give her some time.'

His voice was extremely level. 'What does that mean?'

'It might make her...recovery slower if she knew that you and I were...close. And I've never lied to her. I can't start now.' As he remained silent, she said, 'She's my *child*! I can't...I *can't* hurt her like that. I know it's a lot to ask,' her hands unconsciously clamped themselves together in her lap, 'but can we wait...until she's able to cope with it?'

'Supposing that never happens?' Kyle asked her. 'What then?'

Fler's face was white. He'd just put her very worst fear into words. 'Then I'll come to you,' she whispered. She couldn't ask Kyle to put his life—their life—on hold forever. Tansy wasn't a little girl any more. Some time she had to take responsibility for herself. 'You say,' she offered. 'You tell me when it's time enough.'

'And if I say now? Now is time enough, I won't wait any longer for you, for *us*?'

Fler closed her eyes, shaking. She felt sick. Was he really asking that of her? A judgement of Solomon? She saw Tansy's white, bewildered face behind her closed lids, heard again the wavering, childish plea, '*I need help*!'

She opened her eyes, wide with pain, and found Kyle on his knees before her, taking her hands in his warm ones, holding them tightly. 'Don't answer that!' he said. 'It was brutally unfair, and I didn't mean it.'

She saw pain in his eyes equal to her own, and heard him say, 'I'll wait, Fler. As long as it takes. I'd wait forever, for you. Because I want, eventually, to live my life with you. To marry you. That's worth waiting for. And I hope that one day you'll love a child of mine as much as you love Tansy.'

'Yours?' She was nearly thirty-eight; she'd given up the thought of more children.

Sudden uncertainty in his face, he said swiftly, 'Not if you feel you don't want a second family. If it's too much to ask of you. I'm sorry, I didn't think.'

'No,' she said, tears shimmering in her eyes, blurring her vision. 'I would *love* to have your child. Our child. If it's not too late.' Lots of women had children in their thirties, even forties. It wasn't so unusual these days.

His fingers gently touched the moisture on her cheeks. 'Don't cry,' he begged. 'Come here.'

She went into his arms and let him kiss away the tears. She pressed hot little kisses of her own on his cheek and along the line of his jaw. And then their mouths met almost accidentally, and they exchanged a long kiss of sweet promise.

Kyle eased her down on to the carpet, lay propped on his elbow as he looked at her, a finger gently tracing the contours of her face, her parted lips. 'This waiting,' he said, 'isn't going to be easy.'

'I know.' She caught his hand and held the back of it to her cheek. 'For either of us. Thank you, Kyle.'

'For what?' He bent and put his lips to her throat, slid them up to the shallow groove below her ear, touched them to her lips.

'For understanding,' she said. 'For being patient.'

'I don't feel very patient,' he said. He ran his hand slowly down her body, over the tantalising mound of her breast, into the concavity of her waist, smoothing the skirt over her hip, his gaze following the lingering exploration. 'That daughter of yours had better get herself straightened out pretty soon. Kiss me once more, and then I'll send you home, before I lose all my self-control.'

Four months later, when Tansy was home for a weekend, she came into her mother's room one night holding a small, bulky volume that she handed to Fler. 'I'd like you to read this,' she said. 'I've been going over it a lot this week.'

'Your diary?' Fler ran a hand over the cover, looking at the gold lettering, 'Three-year diary'.

'I thought it would be cool to have one for my whole time at university,' Tansy said. 'But now I don't think I'll finish it. Read it tonight, could you?'

'You're sure you want me to?'

'I'm sure. And tomorrow, we'll burn it.'

She kissed Fler's cheek and went back to her own room.

It was all there. Her first meeting with Kyle, her naïve admiration, turning quickly to starry-eyed infatuation. The kiss that she'd found so wonderfully romantic, that had set her off dreaming of future dates, further kisses that had never materialised. And then the rationalisations. Kyle couldn't overtly court her because of his position, couldn't meet her outside of the university in case they were seen. He deliberately ignored her in class because if their 'relationship' were known it might affect his career. She'd written down every word he'd ever spoken to her, and they were pitifully few, yet she'd managed to weave them into a fantasy of frustrated love on both their parts. When she threw herself at his head only to be gently repulsed, she'd decided that his scruples didn't allow him to take her virginity, and adored him all the more. His attempt to tell her that her feelings were a youthful stage that she'd grow out of was interpreted as a chivalrous declaration that he'd wait for her to grow up. And she'd pathetically tried to hasten the process. Everything he said and did was contorted to conform to the fairytale she'd concocted in her mind.

Once or twice Fler couldn't help but laugh, even as her heart was wrenched with pity. None of it had been funny for poor Tansy. Nor for Kyle, caught in the ever-tightening net of an adolescent obsession.

'You see,' Tansy said in the morning, still in her nightshirt, sitting with her legs twined under her on the end of Fler's bed, 'I just didn't want to believe that he was really turning me down. I can't explain why, but it was just so *important* to me that he wanted me, too. I think I had myself half-convinced that we *had* been having an affair. Or at least that we were about to.' She grimaced. 'I was so-o pathetic! Pat was right. I was really turning into a nut-case.'

'Why did you want me to read it?' Fler asked.

'I thought...maybe you needed to. You haven't seen Kyle lately, have you?'

Fler's breath seemed to stop. 'Not for a while.'

Too casually, Tansy said, 'Why don't you invite him up for a weekend or something? The house isn't full at this time of year.'

A leap of longing, of hope, was replaced by a sudden leaden foreboding. 'Why?'

'*Why*?' Tansy looked at her in astonishment. 'You told me you love him!'

Fler swallowed. 'Yes,' she said. 'I do.'

'Well, then...don't you want to see him?' As Fler still hesitated, Tansy added impatiently, '*I* won't be here! This isn't some ploy to get him back, you know. I mean, get him for myself.'

Gently, Fler said, 'Is it some ploy to make amends, then?'

Tansy flushed, giving her a lopsided little smile. 'I've been a real pain to you both, haven't I? I'd like to do *something* to make up for it. Supposing he finds someone else?'

'There's no hurry,' Fler told her. 'And he isn't looking for anyone else.'

Just two months after that, Tansy stood by as her bridal attendant when Fler married Kyle Ranburn in the small white church.

Afterwards she kissed her mother, and stood on tiptoe to kiss Kyle's cheek, too. 'Thanks, Mum,' she said, standing back, 'for giving me the handsomest stepfather in town.'

Kyle smiled back at her. 'Thank *you*. For the compliment and for allowing me to share your mother's love. Where's your friend?'

'Pat? Oh, he's around. I think he has plans to shower you both with confetti, but I told him it's not allowed in the church. He'll be lurking round some doorway.'

'She's very casual about him,' Kyle remarked some hours later, lying on a hotel bed, his tie discarded and his shirt undone. He was watching Fler brush her hair. 'But I think they're fond of each other.' He and Fler had seen quite a lot of Pat and Tansy lately, usually together.

'He's in love with her,' Fler said. 'But I think Tansy's a bit wary of getting in too deep with anyone. And Pat's very sensibly playing it cool. They're young, they have plenty of time.' Fler smoothed on some lipstick and said, 'Are you taking me to dinner looking like that?'

'I've a better idea,' Kyle told her.

Fler's eyes met his in the mirror. 'Oh?' She put down the lipstick and got up to wander over to the bed, looking down at him. 'What's that?'

'This.' His hand shot out to grab her wrist and pull her down on top of him. He took her head in his hands, mussing her newly brushed hair, and brought her freshly painted mouth to his.

'And this,' Kyle said moments later, sliding down the zip at the back of her dress. 'And this.' His fingers deftly parted the catch of her bra.

'I just put that back on,' she protested.

'Well, take it off again.' He turned over, pinning her beneath him, her head against the pillow.

Fler laughed, and linked her hands around his neck. 'You take it off.' She leaned forward to kiss his mouth, languorous, slow.

'Delighted,' he said, when they surfaced. He eased the dress from her shoulders and slid down the straps underneath.

'For an intellectual,' she said to the top of his dark head, while delicious little thrills of sensation emanated from the path his mouth was taking, 'you seem to have a very limited range of ideas.'

He raised his face from her breasts and said, 'Oh, yeah? Well, let me introduce you to a few more.'

He shifted his position, and she said, laughing, 'Kyle, what are you——? *Kyle*!'

An hour or so later he said, 'Any more complaints?'

'None,' she said breathlessly, stroking his bare back. 'If I did, I might never get my dinner.'

'I'm a selfish swine,' he said. 'You must be starved. I'll take you to dinner. And afterwards——'

'Afterwards,' Fler said firmly, 'I'll show you that it isn't only you ivory-tower types who have ideas. I promise you,' she added, her lips teasing his ear as she murmured seductively into it, 'that I have a few interesting ones of my own.'

POSTCARDS FROM EUROPE

HARLEQUIN PRESENTS™

Hi!

I should be on cloud nine. Rolf Felder asked me to marry him. He's the handsome owner of a hotel chain here in Switzerland, but I'm not convinced he'll ever view our marriage as anything more than one of convenience. I'm desperately in love with him—what should I do?     Love, Abigail

Travel across Europe in 1994 with Harlequin Presents. Collect a new Postcards From Europe title each month!

Don't miss
NO PROMISE OF LOVE
by Lilian Peake
Harlequin Presents #1700

Available in November wherever Harlequin Presents books are sold.

HPPE11

Relive the romance.... This December,
Harlequin and Silhouette are proud to bring you

by Request™

# Little Matchmakers

All they want for Christmas is a mom *and* a dad!

Three complete novels by your favorite authors—
in one special collection!

**THE MATCHMAKERS** by Debbie Macomber
**MRS. SCROOGE** by Barbara Bretton
**A CAROL CHRISTMAS** by Muriel Jensen

When your child's a determined little matchmaker,
*anything* can happen—especially at Christmas!

Available wherever
Harlequin and Silhouette books are sold.

HARLEQUIN® Silhouette®

HREQ1194

## EDGE OF ETERNITY
### Jasmine Cresswell

Two years after their divorce, David Powell and Eve Graham met again in Eternity, Massachusetts—and this time there was magic between them. But David was tied up in a murder that no amount of small-town gossip could free him from. When Eve was pulled into the frenzy, he knew he had to come up with some answers—including how to convince her they should marry again...this time for keeps.

**EDGE OF ETERNITY,** available in November from Intrigue, is the sixth book in Harlequin's exciting new cross-line series, **WEDDINGS, INC.**

Be sure to look for the final book, **VOWS,** by Margaret Moore (Harlequin Historical #248), coming in December.

WED6

# HARLEQUIN®

## PRESENTS Plus

Madeleine's family won't let her forget the scandal she caused when she was engaged to Dominic Stanton. And now that she's back after a four-year absence, Dominic won't let her forget the passion they shared!

Vito di Cavalieri had abandoned Ashley just when she needed him most. Now Vito is back in her life, clearly believing that it was *she* who betrayed him. And that revenge is his due...

Fall in love with Dominic and Vito—Madeleine and Ashley do!

Watch for

*Passionate Scandal* by Michelle Reid
Harlequin Presents Plus #1695

and

*A Vengeful Passion* by Lynne Graham
Harlequin Presents Plus #1696

Harlequin Presents Plus
The best has just gotten better!

Available in November wherever Harlequin books are sold.

PPLUS18

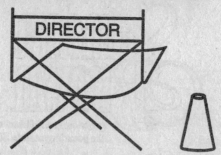

# HOLLYWOOD

### DIRECTOR

## Coming this Fall—
## Harlequin Movies on TV!

If you like a good romance you'll *love* the brand-new Harlequin movies that will be airing on the CBS network on Sunday afternoons this Fall!

These full-length *romantic* movies are based on Harlequin novels written by some of your favorite authors! They're entertaining romances with lots of twists and turns and guaranteed to keep you riveted to your seat, so watch for them!

As a Reader Service member you'll be hearing more about these Harlequin movies in the months to come. Next month's *Heart to Heart* newsletter, for example, will bring you more specific details, along with information about the exciting prizes you could win in the all new

### "Harlequin Goes to Hollywood" Sweepstakes!

CBSBPA

This November, share the passion with *New York Times* Bestselling Author

# Sandra Brown

(previously published under the pseudonym Erin St. Claire)

in

# THE DEVIL'S OWN

Kerry Bishop was a good samaritan with a wild plan. Linc O'Neal was a photojournalist with a big heart.

Their scheme to save nine orphans from a hazardos land was foolhardy at best—deadly at the worst.

But together they would battle the odds—and the burning hungers—that made the steamy days and sultry nights doubly dangerous.

**Reach for the brightest star in women's fiction with**

## MIRA™

MSBDO-R